The Raton Rustlers

THE RATON RUSTLERS

Roy Wayne

AVALON BOOKS
THOMAS BOUREGY AND COMPANY, INC.
NEW YORK

© Copyright 1984 by Roy Wayne
Library of Congress Catalog Card Number: 84-91641
ISBN: 0-8034-8440-2

PRINTED IN THE UNITED STATES OF AMERICA
BY HADDON CRAFTSMEN, SCRANTON, PENNSYLVANIA

For my
granddaughter, Jessica

Chapter One

Dan Martin squirmed on the stagecoach seat. His too-tight shirt collar chafed against his freshly shaven neck. The store-bought suit was ill fitting on his lean, six-foot frame. A derby was squeezed down over his short brown hair.

Dang, he thought, being a range detective sure had its drawbacks. Now why had his boss, Captain Franklin, ordered him to dude up and enter town on the stage?

He fidgeted with a notebook and pretended to jot down a few lines. The coach jolted over a rut in the rough main street, causing the point of his stubby pencil to break.

Martin muttered an invective. He pocketed the pencil and snapped his notebook shut.

1

This must be some hush-hush assignment, he thought, for Captain Franklin to want him disguised as an Eastern newspaper reporter.

He tugged at the uncomfortable high collar and caught a faint smile of derision from a rugged cowman. Martin hunched his wide shoulders, glaring at the man.

The cowman grimaced as the stagecoach slid to a bone-jarring halt.

Dan Martin almost tumbled out of his seat at the sudden stop. He hastily pulled himself together and politely waited until the other passengers had alighted. He stepped down and eyed the single dusty main street of Clayton, New Mexico Territory.

The raw cowtown offered little. He hid a grunt of disgust and claimed his two carpet-bags. One held his few possessions: gun belt, range clothes, and assorted items. The other only contained some crumpled-up newspapers.

He crossed the busy main street, barely avoiding a group of skylarking cowboys. He casually sauntered into the Cattlemen's Hotel, with its cowhide furniture. He paused just inside the lobby, trying for all the world to look the part of a bewildered Easterner. Then he approached the desk.

An indifferent clerk passed him the register and he wrote, "Dan Martin, New York City."

Martin hid a secret grin at that. Heck, he had never been east of the Mississippi River.

The clerk snorted. Another dang dude underfoot. As if he didn't have enough worries, what with the territorial governor in town.

"Second floor. Your room is the first one to the right," he said and pushed a key over the counter.

"Thank you." Martin accepted the key, striving to keep up his act. He picked up the carpetbags and hurried upstairs.

The unfamiliar low-cut shoes hurt his feet. He hit the top step and tripped.

Martin could hear the clerk's dry chuckle. Shoot, wasn't anything going to work out? Here he was, not supposed to attract any attention. But it seemed every time he made a move something went wrong. It had to be the darn dude getup, he told himself.

At first the key would not work. Martin shrugged resignedly and jammed it in the lock one more time. The door swung inward. He sighed. The dad-gummed thing hadn't been locked in the first place!

Martin tossed the bags aside and kicked the door shut. He took off the offensive derby and wiped the sweat from his forehead, then sat down on the narrow bed.

His eyes idly rested on the dirty window. Age-yellowed curtains hung limp, not quite meeting in the middle.

Finally, figuring no one could see into the dim room, he produced a letter from an inside pocket. It had been sent by Captain Franklin. Dan Martin read its puzzling contents for the dozenth time.

It was dated Santa Fe, June 2, 1889, and it was short.

Dress like an Eastern newspaperman. Be in Clayton on noon stage next Friday. Register at the Cattlemen's Hotel. Wait four hours, then bring pencil and paper to room 24. If asked, you have come to interview the Governor. I'm shorthanded and desperate. Don't let me down.

Martin tucked the letter away in a vest pocket. He groaned inwardly. A hunger pain gnawed at his guts.

Sighing, the inexperienced range detective sallied forth to find an eatery.

The meal seemed to take an eternity. But then, he had loads of time. He endured the roughly dressed cattlemen's baiting, knowing it was just in fun. The stiff collar became almost unbearable.

Martin returned to his room at the hotel. He took a nap, then paced the floor, consulting a long-stemmed watch. Finally, it was time. Now, he thought, maybe the captain would explain all of this.

Governor Trimble eyed the lanky man in the baggy pants and too-tight coat. He cast a quizzical look at Captain Franklin, head of the Territorial Rangers.

"Have a seat, Dan," Captain Franklin said.

Governor Trimble studied the dude before him. He turned back to Franklin with an angry glow in his eyes. "Is this the best excuse for a range detective that you have?"

Captain Franklin spread wide his hands. "Don't let this city getup fool you, Governor. Martin has been with us for over two years and not failed on an assignment yet. I'll grant you, he has some unorthodox methods, but they seem to work."

Governor Trimble relented. "Good with a gun, eh?"

"Very fast," Captain Franklin put in before Martin could answer. "Another thing. Nobody seems to take him serious, and the next thing they know, he has the goods on them."

"I see. I think," Trimble said in a brusque tone.

"Do you mind telling me something, Captain?" Martin asked. "What is this all about?"

"Well, Dan, the governor will fill you in on the gist of the trouble," Franklin answered.

Trimble nodded his head. "Here is the deal, Martin. There have been several reports of rustling coming in from up around Raton. Also a shooting. And then the deputy assigned there, he up and quit.

"He didn't give any reason, but we think maybe he was scared off. What we need is someone no one will suspect to ride in, latch onto a riding job with one of the local outfits, and scotch this before big trouble develops."

"Uh-huh. Usual game," Dan Martin murmured.

"Little more this time," Franklin put in. "Anyhow, an old ridin' pard of mine runs the Rafter W. Seems they are the hardest hit for some reason."

"I reckon that spread will be the place to start," Martin said. "When do you want me to get going?"

Captain Franklin said, "Tonight. When it's

dark, I'll have a broomtail and a beat-up saddle rig waiting at the north end of town where the trail branches. You dress like a down-in-the-heels cowboy. Take a few days to get to Raton. Ride in needing a shave. Do your best to appear no more than just a cowpoke. An out-of-work drifter."

"That's easy." Martin grinned. "Wasn't much more than that when you took me on."

The governor's fingers drummed a tattoo on the bed post. His craggy eyebrows arched together as the young range detective shut the door after himself.

"Franklin, are you sure that man is good enough?" he growled.

"Believe it or not, he is one of the best. I guarantee that when he rides into Raton no one will ever think twice about him," Franklin assured the governor.

"You better be right, Franklin. My reappointment comes up soon and I cannot afford to have a range war develop out of this trouble."

Franklin waved a hand. "Martin will handle this. His nondescript appearance will cover any movements that he makes."

"I hope you're right. If he fails and I'm not

reappointed, then your job is on the line as well."

"I fully understand that," Franklin murmured. A large chuckle escaped his rather generous mouth.

"What do you find so funny about this?" Trimble growled.

"Just thinkin' about old Howlin' Winters and his bunch of daughters. I thought about warning Martin about them, but figured it would be more natural if he found out firsthand after he lands on the Rafter W."

That brought a dry chuckle from deep within Trimble's massive chest. A wide grin slowly split his lips. "Oh, boy!" he exploded. "Just wait till he tangles with April. Kinda wish I could be there and see the fun.

"Seriously, Franklin, do you think he can catch on with the Rafter W?" The light died in Trimble's eyes.

"I'm banking on it. Latest word has it that they're shorthanded account of this trouble," Franklin replied.

Trimble produced a bottle and two glasses from the top dresser drawer. He poured out two fingers each. "Here's to your man's success," he said.

Franklin raised his drink. "And your reappointment."

Dan Martin returned to his room. He flopped down on the rickety bed. Dust rose and tickled his nostrils. A fit of sneezing interrupted his thoughts.

It was several moments before the sneezing stopped and he could think straight. His first problem was to leave this place unobtrusively. The Eastern dude he pretended to be had to disappear from the face of the earth.

He cast a speculative gaze at the dirty window and noticed that the sun was lowering. Already, long shadows were beginning to gather.

Well, first he'd have himself a leisurely supper. Then he'd come back to his room, take his bags downstairs, and check out. He could tell the hotel clerk that he had interviewed the governor, so there was no more reason to stay in this small cowtown. He'd say some friends from the next town were picking him up in a buggy later tonight. And that was what the clerk would believe. Then he would promptly forget all about the Eastern dude...

*   *   *

Dark shadows shrouded the trail. The scrubby sorrel switched his tail. He rolled big eyes at Dan Martin's strange antics.

The derby came off with a decided yank. The low-cut shoes were next. This brought a sigh of gratification from the footsore Martin.

"Dad-gum," he muttered. "Cap Franklin didn't tell me it was goin' to be such a long hike out here. Darn him, anyway."

Dan Martin rummaged around in the filled carpetbag, feeling for his real clothes in the dark. He swiftly changed into his range duds and slipped into the worn but comfortable boots.

"Now, what can I do with this dude getup? Sure don't want to be seen packing it on the trail," Dan grumbled.

He cuffed back his battered old stetson, debating the situation. The sorrel stamped and Dan's head swiveled around.

But now the sorrel stood head down, uninterested in the man's problem. An owl hooted. Dan stirred into motion.

Leading the horse, he tramped through the dark and, upon moving into an extra-thick clump of brush, he paused. "Uh-huh. This might be all right," he grunted, ground-hitching the animal.

Using his hands and some twigs, he dug a hole, shoved the bags in, then covered them. He spread leaves and dead twigs on top. A mild invective escaped his mouth when a limb bent back and slapped against his ear.

The night lightened with the arrival of a quarter moon. Dan Martin tightened the cinch on the old battered hull. He toed aboard the sorrel gelding and gave him a whack on the neck.

"Gid-dap, Hoss. Time we headed out," he said softly.

An irrelevant thought brought a low chuckle from the rider. "You sure are a scrub, all right. Cap Franklin probably got paid to take you off somebody's hands. Now you remind me of a time down Deming way when that Mexican lady wanted me to disguise my horse. Talk about a wild idea. I had a plug just about like you then."

Martin clucked to the slow-moving sorrel. He then fell silent, intently studying the trail ahead.

Dry leather squeaked as the old saddle protested under his weight. This occasional noise and the sorrel's dragging hooves were the only sounds to break into his quiet thoughts.

He dozed in the saddle. The miles slowly

dropped away. Dawn came and the lone rider awoke with a start.

A tiny stream trickled under the sorrel's dripping muzzle. Dan stretched in the saddle. His back ached from the plug's racking gait.

He stepped out of the saddle with a low groan. "Good a place as any to camp, I reckon, Hoss. I 'spose you'd like that hull off as much as I'm glad to be out of it."

His fingers worked at the cinch. A happy snort rewarded his efforts when the saddle slipped from the sorrel's back.

Dan spread his bedroll under a stand of low-hanging willows. He stretched out and pulled his hat down to cover his face.

Moments later a soft snore punctuated the surrounding stillness.

Chapter Two

Dan rode into the outskirts of Raton on the trail-weary sorrel. A huge black-butted Colt .45 was slung low and tied to his leg. Other than the big revolver, there didn't seem to be anything unusual about the stranger in the shabby clothes.

A dark growth of whiskers denoted many days on the trail. He sat slack in a worn saddle. A lumpy bedroll rested behind him, and the stock of a rifle protruded from the saddle skirt.

The rider appeared to be somewhere in his middle twenties. His untrimmed brown hair poked out from under a shabby, misshapen hat. His boots were dusty and run-down at the

13

heels. One boot looked to be patched.

He reined the sorrel aside and paused a moment before riding on. He studied the long, dusty main street that bisected the thriving cowtown.

It was Saturday afternoon and payday for the outlying ranches. Several cowboys sauntered down the plank sidewalk. A wagon pulled away from the general store. A half dozen or so old men loafed on the front porch of a tall false-fronted hotel. A group of riders dismounted across the street from the hotel and swaggered into the Longhorn Saloon.

The seedy-looking drifter idly reached into his shirt pocket and pulled out a sack of Bull Durham. His hand stopped as he noticed the squat jail directly across the street from where he sat.

Bright sunlight glinted from its steel bars. A tall, grizzled old man stood framed in the doorway. A shaft of sun danced and played over his highly polished badge.

Marshal McCoy cast a speculative gaze over the stranger and promptly dismissed him as just another drifting cowboy hitting the grub line. He found nothing in the man's ragged appearance to stir his interest. McCoy heeled around and disappeared into his office.

Dan Martin placed a bit of tobacco onto the thin cigarette paper. He twirled the tiny paper cylinder and licked it together.

Then he placed the brown cylinder in his mouth and raked a match over his gun butt. The match flared and soon a stream of thin blue-gray smoke came from his nostrils.

Dan gigged the sorrel and headed for the Longhorn Saloon. He rode past the general store just as a fairly large, rawboned figure came out.

At first he thought the stocky redheaded figure was a man. The head turned and thrust an iron jaw in his direction. Slitted green eyes blazed forth, showing an evil temper.

Dan could not help but be surprised. This was no man, he now saw, but the toughest, homeliest woman on two legs. She was so hard-looking, it made his eyes ache.

Dan broke into a grin and quickly looked away, afraid this apparition would do further injury to his sore eyes.

"What in the Hades are you snickering at?" the woman demanded.

Dan tugged his battered old hat down. "Nothin', ma'am. Nothin' at all." He slapped the sorrel into a faster gait.

* * *

Spring Winters stood inside the store, near the front window, debating whether or not to buy the frilly hat that was on display. She picked up the hat and stepped to the door, intending to ask April's opinion, not that it mattered much. April couldn't care less about pretty hats and such. But she was always ready to air her thoughts.

Spring stopped short as a down-at-the-heels puncher rode by. April's words to the man scarcely registered, but Spring's heart leaped when she saw his impish grin and heard his low-voiced answer. Spring felt a sudden warm glow move through her and wondered why.

For the rider had not shaved for some time and seemed a bit shabby looking, a little more shabby looking than most.

His voice lingered in her ears, though. Suddenly, Spring thought, Oh, my gosh, what is the matter with me?

A petulant frown briefly creased her pretty face. It could not be denied that Spring Winters was a fine-looking young woman. She was slightly over five feet tall and was well-proportioned. Short-cropped, curly black hair framed a heart-shaped face. Her skin was smooth and nicely tanned.

Spring had just turned twenty. But although she was lovely, the eligible young men all seemed to avoid her. Until this year it had never worried her. Now she daydreamed about love and marriage.

Only, she had to wait her turn. April ran the ranch with May to back her up. April, May, and June were older than Spring, but all through the years the handling of the household chores and all the buying of supplies had fallen upon Spring's shoulders. And somehow the men around Raton had gotten the wrong idea that she was like April.

Then there were her two younger sisters. Summer was now eighteen and blossoming into a beautiful auburn-haired young woman. But Summer was a tomboy!

Little Autumn was the one that really worried Spring. Not yet sixteen, Autumn was a tiny-waisted, vivacious blonde. Her face still held a smidgen of cute freckles that set off a pert nose and full, pouting lips.

Spring heaved a sigh, came to a decision, and placed the hat with her other purchases. She could still feel her heart pounding extra fast.

April came inside, dusting flour off her vest. An angry glare lit her pale green eyes. She muttered a low invective.

"Now, April! Don't ever let Father hear you talking like that," Spring admonished.

"Right now I don't give a hoot what Pa has to say." April's deep voice came out harsh and angry. "Them lazy riders of ours are all too darn proud to do anything but sit on a horse. Every dang one of them are up at the Longhorn soakin' down the swill. Not one offered to help, so here I have to go and load up all the grub. Heck, I ought to let them go hungry next month."

"You don't mean that!" Spring gasped, faking amazement.

Every payday it was the same. April actually loved to show up the men when it came to work. But she was just like the riders when it came right down to the tedious chores like fence-mending and cleaning out the corrals.

Spring smiled slightly. "Any luck on hiring a handyman? I need more firewood for the house, and there are about a million things that need to be fixed."

"No, darn it. Nobody wants to work at them things anymore. I sure wish Pa would stay home and tend to the chores. Sometimes I think his preachin' is just an excuse to get out of workin' a little now and then."

Spring said, "Well, maybe the boys will run

across somebody. I heard you mention it to them."

"Meanwhile, I do everything," April said. "Tote the flour and all. Now I have to talk to Stanley Ross."

A splintered hitchrail fronted the saloon. Dan Martin found a space and reined in beside two cow ponies with a Rafter W brand on their hips. From across the street he could hear the tail end of several loud laughs.

He cast a furtive glance at the loafers just as one pointed down the street and slapped his knee. Dan followed the man's gaze and his jaw went slack.

Danged if that big, mean-looking female wasn't carrying a hundred-pound sack of flour without any visible strain. She tossed it into the back of a wagon and walked back for another sack.

Dan stepped onto the boardwalk. He looked all around as he brushed off his pants. He hitched up his sagging gun belt and sauntered into the saloon.

It was dim and cool inside the place. Dan moved nonchalantly across the boxlike interior. The pleasant odor of fresh sawdust assailed his nose.

The big Colt .45 felt snug and heavy on his hip as he bellied up to the bar. He quietly ordered a beer.

A swift sideways shift of his eyes caught a tall rider watching him quizzically. Dan thumbed back his hat.

"Say, partner. You seem kinda down and out. Lookin' for a job?" the rider asked.

"Sure am," Dan said.

The other man nudged a loose-jointed cowboy with his elbow. "Tell you what, pard. My handle is Chuck Raines. This fella here is Jack Lester, top bronc-stomper for the Rafter W. You stick with us, and when we get back to the ranch, I'll introduce you to the boss."

Dan could hardly believe this kind of luck. A job at the Rafter W was just what he wanted. The ranch would be his base for a time while he scouted for the rustlers.

"Hey, barkeep! Give us another round," Chuck Raines said. Then he turned to Dan. "Miss April, she bosses the range, said just this mornin' that she could use another hand on the place. We been sort of keepin' an eye peeled for the right man." A friendly but mischievous grin crinkled the corners of his eyes.

"Miss April?" Dan frowned. "The Rafter W has a lady boss?" Here was a new wrinkle to the setup. Cap Franklin had not said anything about him having to work for a woman.

"Yep. And she's a good 'un. Her pappy, old Howlin' Winters, owns the spread. He don't do much runnin' of it anymore, though. Spends most of his time ridin' the circuit, preachin'. That's how he come by the front handle of Howlin'," Raines explained.

A chuckle welled up from Jack Lester's thin chest. He straightened his lank form to tower over Raines by a good six inches. And if Dan did not miss his guess, Chuck Raines topped six feet himself.

"You hang around, cowboy. The Rafter W feeds real good. We got an old Chinaman cook, Fong, and he puts out a man-sized meal," Jack Lester said and patted his flat middle. He smiled down amicably at Dan Martin. "Pays good, too," he added.

Chapter Three

After April Winters left his office, Stanley Ross patted his rounding paunch and let a rare chuckle well up in his throat. Dang fool woman was walking, no running, into his net just as fast as she could.

An extension of credit for the Rafter W at his general store suited Ross just fine. He wiped moisture from his balding head and chuckled again.

His plans were beginning to take shape, finally. Ross thought about the past year, since he had arrived in Raton with a sizable roll from his last job. Embezzling several thousand from that St. Louis bank had turned out to be easier than he had anticipated.

And now he owned the only store in this

town and a sizable chunk of the bank also. His palms sweated with greed.

Just a few more months now and the Winters note at the bank would come due. Between it and the rather large bill that April continued to run up at his store, he would soon have the Rafter W in his hands.

Stanley Ross, banker and upstanding businessman. That thought made the rotund man's stomach jiggle with mirth. Now if Buck Shedd and his men were to run off another small jag of Rafter W stock, it would keep them occupied and hanging around until he put the final touches to his long-range plans.

Ross well remembered the day he had stepped out of the stage and right into a big Fourth of July celebration. Now that was some kind of a shindig, he recalled.

Just a few more weeks now, and the entire countryside would be in town for another Fourth. That would be the time for Shedd to strike. The boys could clean out Adam Brewer's Circle B and sweep the Rafter W's north range clean. What Shedd did with the drive, Ross didn't care.

Both outfits would be flat busted with no stock to sell off. And all he had to do was step in with some papers and take them over.

Ross thought of Buck Shedd and the ragtag bunch of outlaws that rode with him. Shedd he had known many years before, and the man could always be bought. That had been a stroke of good luck, running into him here at Raton. For after this job was over, Buck would take his money and drift. Anyway, he only thought that Ross wanted the combined ranges that belonged to Winters and Brewer.

Put the two together and they would make a fine spread, Ross thought. But, no, he didn't want anything to do with raising cows. The dumb brutes. Not enough quick money there.

Ross wiped off his sweaty palms with a clean handkerchief. Sure was a big, fine stand of timber back on those north slopes, he mused. Now if a sawmill were placed along that sweeping bend in Turkey Creek up above the Canadian River, that would be something.

But that was still not all that Stanley Ross wanted from the Rafter W. An evil grin spread over his thick mouth. Meaty jowls twitched as he reviewed his plans.

It would be more than a pleasure to boot April Winters off the ranch. But that June Winters was something else.

How well he remembered the years right

after the Civil War. He was a young man then and, although already going bald and with a pudgy body, he had thought of himself as quite a ladies' man.

He had packed a carpetbag and gone South hoping to make a fortune from the strife-torn land. Continually rebuffed by the beautiful Southern belles, he had vowed that one day he would show those aristocratic ladies a thing or two, he would.

Now, that June Winters surely reminded him of those haughty young women that he had suffered so many indignities from. With the ranch in his hands, Ross planned to offer June a way to still live gracefully.

He would be extremely wealthly. She would jump at the chance to be his wife and have an elegant home. And an aristocratic wife such as she would make could be a boon to his political plans.

Once more it crept into the back of his mind that this territory would someday be a state. Then he, Stanley Ross, just might be elected governor.

Ross consulted his pocket watch and, finding the hour somewhat late, strolled out of his office. With a rather pompous air, he said,

"Lock up, Hawkins. I'll see you tomorrow."

"Yes, sir, Mr. Ross," the aging store clerk said.

Ross paused on the sidewalk to light a cigar. He puffed thoughtfully for a moment, then decided to make his usual nightly visit to the Longhorn Saloon. He started to head up the street when a lean figure detached itself from the shadows and fell into step by his side.

The storekeeper gave a slight start. He frowned at the dim form.

"Gettin' jumpy, Ross?" The man kept his voice low, but it held a slight sarcastic note.

Ross breathed a silent curse. "Shedd, how many times must I tell you not to be seen with me?"

"Quiet tonight." Buck Shedd paced shoulder to shoulder with Ross. "Anybody asks, tell 'em that I hit you up for a loan or credit at the store."

"What do you want?" Ross asked as they passed through a yellow light shining from the Raton beanery. He caught a sneering grin on Buck Shedd's hard face.

"Been doin' a lot of thinkin' about this deal we got, Ross. Appears like me and the boys are doin' all the hard work and you're sittin' back gettin' fat. Now, me for one, I don't really care, but Carl Tucker and Bud Stone are startin' to ask questions. Tim Alvin and Tom Vernell are gettin' edgy. Can't say for sure just yet what Al Hayes wants." Shedd motioned to a dark alleyway. "Let's slip in here and jaw for a minute."

Ross tossed away his cigar in disgust, but quickly followed Shedd for a short distance into the dark alley. "Why here?" he whined.

"Because my horse is tied down at the end. And, besides, we don't want to run into Marshal McCoy, now do we?" Shedd's low voice still held its sarcastic cutting edge.

He stabbed a stiff finger into Ross's stomach and felt the fat man flinch. "Now you listen and hear me real good, Ross. Like I said, I've been doin' a lot of thinkin'. I'm tired of runnin', always on the move. This scheme of yours shapes up bigger to me than just penny-ante rustlin'. I want a bigger cut. I figure you are plannin' on takin' over the Rafter W, but when?"

"Soon now," Ross promised. "You boys run off another small jag in a few days, then lay low. I'll let you know in a few weeks when to hit, and hit hard and fast. One big drive." His voice rose at the thought of the culmination of his carefully laid plans.

"Keep your voice down," Shedd cautioned. "You want the whole town to hear? Now what's in this for me?"

"Money, Buck. I'll have a buyer lined up and ready to take delivery at Durango. No questions asked. You split with the boys any way you feel like. Then you can drift down towards Mexico with a full wallet."

"Uh-huh. You don't hear so good. Not enough," Shedd hissed. "I want half of the ranch."

Ross stood stock-still pondering this for a minute. Half the ranch. He groaned inwardly. For his plans to work, the Rafter W had to be bled dry before their fall roundup and drive to market.

But if Shedd got control of half the ranch, he would soon find out about the timber. Yeah, Ross thought, when the sawmill and timber jacks started to arrive. Then Shedd would demand half the money from the lumbering operation. And a partner with Buck Shedd's reputation would kill any chance that he might have of securing the governor's chair.

"Let me think it over," Ross hedged.

"Take your time," Shedd sneered. "You got one week." He wheeled and vanished into the blackness, leaving Ross with a very troubled mind.

Stanley Ross emerged from the alley's mouth. He cast a furtive glance in both directions before heading for the Longhorn. Now he really needed a stiff drink to steady his nerves.

Shedd would have to be taken care of, Ross thought. He stood at the long bar and took his customary evening drink. Things were pretty quiet for a Saturday night. But even if any of his acquaintances among the tradespeople had been there, Ross would have ignored them.

He remained cool to the bartender's attempt to draw him into conversation. Soon the man tired of the one-sided prattle and moved away to wipe futilely at the already shiny bar.

Ross started to leave the Longhorn Saloon and his eyes traveled over the near-empty room. He hesitated and turned back to stare thoughtfully at a gambler.

The man wore all black except for a white ruffled shirt, Ross noted. And he could not help but think that a derringer hid out somewhere on the gambler's person.

The germ of an idea grew in Ross's fertile brain. Although he let it be known quite openly

that he did not carry a gun, he owned a stingy
little derringer himself.

He hurried out of the saloon. Then he made
his way to the small back room behind the
general store. Here he lived a spartan life.

Buck Shedd was getting too big for his boots,
Ross thought. He dug around in a dilapidated
carpetbag and came out with the small gun.

Ross broke open the little weapon and made
sure that it was loaded. Now what? he wondered, not relishing the idea of carrying it
around in his pocket.

He sat down heavily on a sagging bed and
mulled over the problem of Buck Shedd. The
derringer felt smooth and natural in the palm
of his hand. He fisted the weapon, swinging
it up to bear on an imaginary foe.

Ross repeated the move several times, noting that his meaty hand almost completely
concealed the tiny gun.

Yes. This should work perfectly, Ross decided. A deep-rooted satisfaction brought him
to his feet.

He entered the musty-smelling store and
made his way by feel along its narrow aisles.
Ross reached his darkened office, but still did
not strike a light.

His thoughts centered briefly on the various

revolvers and rifles stocked in the store.

A rifle would be much too awkward. And the short-barreled derringer would swing up out of a desk drawer much easier than the longer-barreled revolvers.

Ross sat down behind his cluttered desk. He opened the top drawer partway and placed the derringer under a stack of papers. He sat still for several moments as if talking to someone.

After a time, he practiced reaching casually into the desk drawer and bringing out the gun. At first the papers interfered with his move. Ross thought about this and finally decided it might be better just to let the weapon sit on top of the papers in the desk for an easier, more sure, draw.

Once again he repeated his moves many times. At last he was completely satisfied.

Now let Buck Shedd come to him. And he surely would, sooner or later, Ross figured. He was now fully prepared.

Nothing would stand in his way of gaining that timber. The ranches of Winters and Brewer were merely penny-ante pawns in his much larger scheme.

Shedd did not fit into his plans after his role of rustler was played out. If Shedd did not, for some reason, come to him, Ross figured to concoct an excuse that would draw him to the office.

Papers to be drawn up and signed maybe? Sure, that would do it. Dangle a deed to the Rafter W before Shedd's nose and he would come running.

Ross heaved his heavy bulk out of the chair. He made his way back to his quarters to retire for the night.

Three days later, Stanley Ross stood by the front window of his store. April Winters had come into town and was now loading a wagon with her many purchases.

Ah, credit. Ross smiled to himself. What a wonderful thing.

His little pig eyes burned with greed. Ross turned to go back to his office. He stopped short, for a strange rider caught his eye. He closely inspected the dust-caked man astride a trail-weary, scrubby sorrel.

No, he quickly decided, this was no outside lawman. Just another drifter. Ross heeled around, satisfied that he would have no trouble with any outside law people here in Raton.

Chapter Four

Dan Martin rode loosely aboard an aging bay mare that belonged to the Rafter W. His ribs hurt from an earlier, jolting fall. The deceptive-looking animal had thrown him that morning.

That had brought great mirth to Jack Lester. But it didn't do Dan's mood much good. He was an awkward cowhand and had bruises from the hard work and from his many mistakes.

Dan studied the fence line and clenched a sore hand. Boy, did that April know how to work a guy.

A gaping hole caught and held his attention. He urged the mare into a faster gait.

Dan approached the fence at an angle. Soon

he could see the broad trail left by hard-driven stock. His lean frame leaned forward in the saddle. He narrowly studied the hoofprints left by at least three riders.

His mood darkened. Now here was brazen rustling. Make a quick gather and bust leather for the hills. His pensive gaze ranged northward.

Towering mountains reared their jagged heads. Nowhere did there seem to be a break.

"They must head up some canyon that leads to Raton Pass," Dan mused aloud. "Now, if I can just nail one of these little sorties, somebody might be persuaded to talk."

Dan's inner senses warned him that this was only a small-scale move. There was more to this rustling Rafter W stock than met the mere eye. He drove the mare in hard pursuit, easily following the plain trail.

Several young steers broke from the bunch. Dutch Otto checked his lathered mount with a vicious curse.

"Let them go," came the stern command from Al Hayes. "We can't afford to lose any more time."

But Dutch Otto was already out of earshot.

He spurred up a side draw, striving to head off the bunch quitters.

One thought only hammered at his single-track mind. Buck Shedd had said to run off fifty head and be damned if that wasn't what he would do.

Hayes cast one last disgusted look after the bulky Dutchman's disappearing figure. He cursed silently and snapped at Tim Alvin, "Keep pushin' 'em hard." He slapped his rope at a lagging steer.

Dan Martin pushed his hard-used mount to her limit. The faint smell of fresh dust hung in the thin air.

But by now it was apparent that the mare was used up. He reined in and dismounted to let her blow.

His fingers automatically fashioned a quirley as he eyed the wide ravine. He was getting close to the rustlers, Dan figured.

His eyes passed over a brush-choked draw. They swung back to study the trail ahead.

A boot toe slowly ground out the quirley. It was time to move on. Dan gathered up the reins.

He started into motion, leading the worn

mare. Brush crackled. A thick voice sounded above the noise.

Suddenly, a wild-eyed steer broke from the draw. Dan jumped, dancing aside to avoid being run down.

The hard-pressed steer brushed by his shoulder. Right on its heels came several more steers breaking out of cover.

There was just enough time to scramble out of their path before a hulking rider spurred into the open. His moon-faced stare showed quick surprise. Wide-spaced eyes, set under craggy brows, studied Dan.

"Hold up. Throw down your gun," Dan ordered.

But Dutch Otto's slow mind had only one thought. A ham-sized hand fisted his Colt. It swept up as he swung towards the waiting cowboy.

Dan dropped swiftly to one knee. He fired, the shot overlaying a burst of smoke from the rustler's Colt.

Otto merely grunted at his first slug's heavy impact. He fired again. Dust jumped at Dan's feet. Tiny particles of rock stung his cheeks and almost blinded him.

Dan blinked away the stinging pain. His

Colt roared once again. Flame spat from the muzzle. Smoke wafted upward. The heavy concussion echoed off a distant hill.

Slowly the huge rustler swayed and toppled from the saddle. He landed with a harsh crunch in the ravine's rocky bottom.

Dan cautiously approached the downed man. But Dutch Otto stared up at the pale blue sky with open, unseeing eyes.

A heavy sigh escaped Dan Martin's lips. There would be no information here, he realized.

The dead outlaw's pockets turned up only the usual. A worn pocketknife with one broken blade. Several small coins and a wallet with parts of a very faded letter. No name, nor anything, though, to tie him to the others.

Dan stood up and glanced around. His own mount was spent and the outlaw's horse had been spooked. It was nowhere to be seen.

Already the tired steers were drifting out of sight, heading for their home range.

No use trying to catch up to the other rustlers, Dan mused, not on the rode-out plug.

He dragged the body under a rocky outcropping and hemmed it in with stones and dirt.

With that chore done, Dan shook off a sickening feeling brought on by the shooting. Might as well head back and start on that dang line fence, he decided.

Anyway, from the way the rustlers were operating, there would be another chance at them.

He rode through the noon hour, and as he warmed to the day, a hunger pain gnawed steadily at his stomach. Dan cursed mildly, this time at himself for forgetting to pack a sandwich.

As he approached a stand of aspens, the whiff of fresh boiling coffee assailed his senses.

Al Hayes heard the Colts' reports echoing up the winding canyon. He reined to a stop, but gestured for Tim Alvin to continue pushing the herd.

Otto was either done for or he had downed a Rafter W cowboy. Al wondered what Buck would think about the shooting, but not for long.

Al slapped his mount back into motion. He did not really care one way or the other about Otto or what Shedd would think.

* * *

Earlier that day Spring had watched the solitary rider grow into a small dot until he finally dipped out of sight behind a low hill. Suddenly, a thought struck her.

Dan had ridden out without packing a lunch. Spring's hands flew to the task. She hurried to wrap several cold beef sandwiches. Then she packed a cup, pot, and a small portion of coffee. She took down a canteen and filled it.

Spring saddled her own horse, thinking, Dan Martin, now is the time I can meet you. It might look obvious, but I don't care. You might not be the greatest cowboy, but that does not matter. And, anyway, I have to talk to you before Autumn.

Spring galloped across the hills, aiming for the badlands. There the long drift fence separated the Rafter W's graze from the deep rocky gullies that bisected their western range.

The wind blew free against her short curls. It put a rosy flush upon her cheeks.

Spring topped a sharp rise. Directly below her stretched the fence. She could see where the posts were down.

She cast a swift look at the sun. Almost noon and surely Dan would ride this way. She chose a sparse stand of aspen just to her right.

Spring wheeled her frisky pinto into the timber. She cleared a circle and ignited a tiny fire. She soon had water boiling.

A handful of coffee grounds went into the pot. Spring watched them rise in the roiling water, then disappear. Her mouth formed a secretive smile.

The muffled fall of hoofbeats reached through the aspens. A dead branch cracked under the hooves.

Spring shoved the coffeepot off the fire. She took off her hat and turned to look up at Dan Martin. Her smile widened.

Dan Martin's eyes held a quizzical look. When he saw Spring smile, his look turned to amazement.

His jaw clenched. Now what was a pretty young filly like this doing way out here? Especially with rustlers and no telling who else ramming around loose.

For this had to be the loveliest creature that he had ever seen. Her eyes held a warmth. A welcoming smile continued to curve her small mouth at the corners. Her tanned cheeks still retained a tinge of red from the wind.

Dan slid out of the saddle. He stepped forward and saw that she was considerably shorter than he was. Even in her jeans and shirt she looked quite shapely.

"Who are you?" Dan asked, finally finding his tongue.

Her smile grew until it seemed to burst over him with its radiance. "Spring Winters. I brought you some lunch and there's fresh coffee. I'll pour you a cup." Her low voice held a thread of excitement. It fell around Dan's ears and captured his heart.

Dan found a seat on an old fallen log. Spring brought a cup of the steaming brew and sat down next to him.

She gazed pensively at the smoldering fire. Her lips were pursed in thoughtful silence. She searched for a way to open the conversation.

"What happened to the fence?" she asked.

Chapter Five

Dan tensed. He silently debated whether or not to tell her about the shootout. Some inner desire to protect her from its harsh reality held him back.

"Rustlers," he replied. "They drove off a small jag early this morning."

"Oh, no, not again," Spring blazed.

"I'm afraid so." Dan tossed out the last dregs of his coffee. "Look, Miss Spring, there's an awful lot of that fence needs tendin' to. Maybe I better get back to it, pronto."

Spring let a slow frown crease her smooth brow. "Don't you like me, Dan?"

"Sure I do, ma'am. Too darn much so. Heck, Miss Spring, I'm just a down-at-the-heels, flat-busted, worthless drifter. Why, I shouldn't even be talkin' to you."

He refrained from just yet mentioning that he was a range detective sent to ferret out the rustling operation.

"Why not, pray tell?" Spring demanded. She hid a shy smile, for she liked to hear his soft drawl touch her ears.

"Ma'am, you're so nice and, well, everything," Dan said. He faltered and was unable to continue. For Spring had flashed another radiant smile at him.

His resolve melted faster than snow in July. He suddenly felt whirled away, having no more chance than a snowball in a fire.

"Please, Dan. Don't call me ma'am or Miss Spring. To you, my name is just Spring. And I like you an awful lot, too. Don't make me out to be somebody I'm not. Dan, I'm just a person. I know this may sound terribly brazen, but I want to be your girl."

"Are you real sure, ma'am? I mean Spring." Dan could scarcely believe his ears. His reeling mind refused to function for a dazed instant.

"Yes, I'm real sure," Spring mimicked. She jumped up. "Let me get you another cup of coffee."

"But that fence." Dan half rose.

"It can wait," Spring said. "You did enough work yesterday for three days. I think it was just mean of April to harass you the way she did."

Dan grinned ruefully. "She sure don't like me. Seems she thought I was laughin' at her the first day in town."

"I know." Spring smiled. "I was in the store and saw you ride by."

"Then you know what I just said is true. I'm just hittin' the grub line between jobs." He hated the lie, but thought it better not to mention being a range detective just yet.

Dan heaved a great sigh. "This—this friendship sure ain't never goin' to work."

"Oh, Dan, give it a chance." Spring spread her hands in a gesture of supplication.

"Shucks, Spring, you and me—it could never lead to anything. The boys told me about your dad and this marryin' business. Each one of you has to wait until all the older sisters are married. There is not a man in his right mind would tie up with April. Beggin' your pardon, her bein' your sister not withstandin'."

"I don't know," Spring mused aloud. "May gave me an idea the other day. If we all scout around, someone might turn up. You know, there are still a lot more men in this country than women."

"Of course, I'll have to get acquainted some first. But I'll put my ear to the ground and see what I can learn," Dan said. His eyes met Spring's and a mutual understanding passed between them...

Dan could feel the sun warm his back. His shadow stretched out long and lean upon the ground. He started to drive in a staple and the head flew off his hammer.

"Aw, heck," Dan muttered. "Time to quit for the day, anyway."

He caught up the mare's reins and toed the stirrup. His hand gripped the saddle, but before he swung aboard, he said, "All right, Betsy. If you act up now, I'll thrash your worthless hide."

The mare just switched her tail. She headed down the trail when his weight settled into the saddle.

Dan labored on the line fence for two more days without any trouble. He was now slowly, but surely, working higher up into the rough hills. Yet he had not picked up any more signs of the rustlers.

Dan rode into the home ranch late that second day. Even before he reached the corrals, a faint ringing sounded. The supper call, and his mouth watered.

He dismounted at the main horse corral and unsaddled Betsy.

Dan walked stiffly towards the cook shack. He cast a furtive glance towards the big ranch house hoping to catch a glimpse of Spring.

No luck. But April was strolling outside. She strode purposefully in his direction.

Dan squeezed down on his tired eyes. Oh, no, he thought. But there was no way out of crossing her path.

April's long jaw was thrust out. Dan squinted a little bit more, trying to keep this vision of sheer ugliness narrowed down.

Her voice lashed out to grate harshly on his harried nerves. "Hold up a minute. Been waitin' for you to get in."

"Yes, ma'am." Dan stopped. He doffed his hat, an automatic gesture. He saw Spring wave from the front porch. His leaden heart rose. Let April try her darnedest. Not even that cantankerous sidewinder could bother him now.

April hitched up her pants. She glowered at the dusty rider. "Aw. Put your hat back on."

Something in April's gruff voice denoted that she seemed in a better mood.

Dan waited for her to continue. Her evident goodwill, although slight, gave him cause for puzzlement. Usually, just the mere sight of him would set her into a frothing rage. He struggled to hide a grin, thankful that the evening shadows covered his face.

"Tomorrow, I want you to take a packhorse and enough supplies to last for a couple of weeks. There's an old cabin further up in the hills. We used to keep it fixed up, using it for a line shack.

"I'm figurin' on doin' that again. Repair what you can around the place. Keep ridin' that fence and turn back any stock that drifts up there. Scout on up higher and see if there are any strays back in those canyons. Gather up what you find and push them back down.

"I haven't decided for sure just yet, but I might send Raines and Lester up there in a week or two. Then you hightail it back down here. There's still a lot of wood-choppin' and general repairs need to be done."

At his nod, April spun on her heel. She stalked away, broad shoulders swinging high in the dusky dark.

Dan ventured another long look at the house, but could not penetrate the gloomy shroud of darkness. A cheerful light splashed out of a window. He waited for several moments, hoping that Spring would be framed in the light. But she failed to show herself and he tramped on to the cook shack.

The next morning Dan Martin finished lashing down a somewhat precarious pack on a swaybacked claybank. It was still early, with the new sun barely breaking over the far hills.

Dan led the bay mare, Betsy, and the claybank to the toolshed. He threw down the lines and stepped into the shed's dim interior.

A trace of perfume tickled his nose. Dan tensed, suddenly afraid that maybe Autumn had waylaid him. For she was disturbingly playful.

"Shush! It's me, Spring." She rested a hand lightly upon his arm.

"I had to see you this morning," she continued. "April doesn't know yet. She would raise the devil."

"What's up?" Dan queried. His tension eased. It was replaced with a warmth at Spring's touch.

"April caught Chuck trying to spark Summer. Then April and May got into an argument. May tried to tell April that she should get married. Boy, did that rile April! She calmed down a little, though, because we received a letter from Father. He said that maybe, if they finished with the church that they are building, he would be home in a week or so," Spring said.

She stopped to catch her breath. Then her voice rushed on in a trembling whisper. "If we try hard to find someone for April, it won't be long. I have to run now. I'll see you when you get back."

Dan remained rooted to the spot for several seconds. Spring's lips suddenly brushed his cheek. Then she quickly slipped outside and vanished.

Spring's last words spurred him into motion. He took some tools that he needed. Then he stepped out of the shed and drew a deep breath, quickly packing the added tools.

The sky was clear. Dan rode high in the saddle. Man, it sure was starting out to be a fine day.

The old slab-and-log cabin leaned downhill slightly. A few chinks were seen between the lower logs. And some repairs had to be made on the roof, but otherwise the place was in reasonable condition.

It didn't take Dan long to clean up the inside. A little mud-and-straw plaster filled the chinks nicely. Two hours of steady hammering and a few extra nails tacked down the roof.

But one complete side of the old peeled log corral was down. Dan could see where several posts had rotted away during their many years in the ground.

He was fortunate in one respect. A new stand of lodgepole pine trees crowded down the slope, ending just shy of the old corral. He eyed their tall, limbless boles for a moment, then picked up the ax. Dan spit once into the palm of his hand and went to work.

Dan lashed the last pole into place. He gave it a little shake and beamed happily at his work.

It had taken him nearly two days of toil to rebuild the corral. But it was worth it, Dan reflected as he stepped back to further survey the product of his labor.

He grunted with satisfaction and cast a critical eye down the line one more time. Not too straight, he thought, but at least it's sturdy enough. He shooed the two horses inside and headed towards the cabin to fix his simple meal.

For some unexplainable reason that evening seemed to drag. He sat outside the musty-smelling cabin, watching the last rays of sunlight spread wide as they refused to let the day end. High overhead a single star already stood out, lonely and forlorn-looking.

Dan watched it moodily for some time. Finally, he muttered, "Shucks. There's no use deludin' myself." He ground out a spent quirley and rose to go to bed.

Dan stretched out and tried to relax his aching muscles. But sleep would not come. He lay staring at the vague shapes of the bare rafters.

I sure have been gettin' off track here, he mused. Maybe I should forget about Spring and concentrate on what I came here for in the first place. Suppose first thing in the mornin' I should head out, but instead of lookin' for strays, it will be a good time to scout for signs of rustlin'. Sure would like to come across those owlhoots' hideout.

Chapter Six

Dan moved up a small creek that was choked with elderberry bushes. This dense wild growth all but obscured the tiny trickle of water. He forced the laboring bay through a particularly thick patch and quite suddenly burst clear of the clawing branches.

The panorama that spread out before him was small, but awe-inspiring. A tiny log cabin nestled under a towering cliff. Stately pines reached to the sky. The open glade wasn't much over two acres in size, but thick, lush grass grew belly high to his horse.

He could see where the creek started from a clear, bubbling spring that gushed out of the ground near the cabin. A pair of fat mules grazed nearby.

While Dan watched, catching his breath, the mules smelled him. One only glanced mildly in his direction and flicked one ear before he resumed grazing.

The other animal, though, was much younger and spooky. He raised a long, wicked head and moved back his ears, defying the intruder to come closer. He pranced forward a few steps, then stopped to snuffle the air. His nostrils flared wide. His lusty bray broke the quietness of the morning, startling Dan's horse into a sidelong step or two.

Dan checked the quivering bay, hauling up roughly on the reins. His ears rang as the braying reverberated around the tiny glen. Slowly, the mocking noise died.

The cantankerous young mule lowered its head and trotted a few steps closer. He stopped near the cabin and again began to bray.

Dan felt sweat break out on his face. He dropped a sweaty palm to the butt of his pistol, wondering if the wild-eyed brute might charge him.

"Don't try it, mister." The voice came from behind Dan. It was harsh to his ears, very similar to the mule's grating bray. The deadly tone held an overlay of ugliness that froze Dan to the saddle.

"Unbuckle your gun belt, then step down slow and easy-like," the unseen man continued.

Dan hesitated, worried that he had stumbled upon a rustler or maybe worse. It could be some outlaw killer hiding out in this rough, almost inaccessible country. His shoulder blades itched. His muscles tightened. He was expecting a bullet to drive into him at any moment.

The cocking of a rifle clicked loud in the utter stillness. It prodded Dan into motion. He fumbled with the buckle on his gun belt. His shoulders sagged and the rig slid down his leg to land with a hushed thump in the tall grass.

Dan swung a leg slowly over his mount's rump and stepped cautiously to the ground. He turned to face the thicket behind him.

Then Dan felt his jaw drop. He openly stared with sheer amazement at the strange sight that shambled out of the brush.

Before him stood a throwback to the mountain men of a hundred years ago. He was extremely tall and slightly stoop shouldered. His age was uncertain. It could be anywhere between thirty and fifty. Long, bony fingers were curled around an old Sharps rifle. His stride

was lithe and springy with youth. Tiny lines
spread out from the corners of his sharp gray
eyes. A cap made of fox skins topped his long
bony head. A foxtail dangled from each side
of the cap. His buckskin shirt and trousers
were greasy and worn shiny with age. And he
wore a sleeveless vest made from wolf pelts.

A smile that could be either friendly or evil
split his matted, tobacco-stained beard. It dis-
played yellow teeth. A gap showed on the bottom row where he had lost a tooth in some
long-forgotten brawl.

The man's face made Dan remember the
livelier mule. He flicked a hasty look over his
shoulder. But the beast had become uninterested and drifted off. Dan swiveled his head
back and caught the man eyeing the brand on
his horse.

"You ride for the Winters brand or did you
steal that hoss?" The eyes remained neutral
but sharp. The man added, talking more to
himself than Dan, "Thought I knowed all them
jaybirds."

Dan finally found his tongue. "I'm new on
the Rafter W. Signed on last week. Name's
Dan Martin."

Slowly the strange man's lips widened into

a fully friendly smile. "Reckon you're all right. Sound honest, anyway. Come on up to the cabin and let's powwow some. Ain't many riders ever come within miles of this place. And you might as well pick up your gun."

Dan walked across the glade. His legs still trembled some and he worried, not sure if the man was in his right mind.

He stepped just inside the small log structure and hesitated.

"Go on in. Make yourself at home."

Dan felt the rifle muzzle prodding at his back. He squinted against the gloomy interior and found a crude homemade table in its very center. Tree stumps were cut chair high at each end of the table. He advanced to the closest one and sat down heavily.

Dan idly noted that the bare dirt floor was tightly packed and swept clean. A single untidy bunk comprised the balance of furnishings in the simple cabin. Wolf pelts and other skins were piled high in one corner. Several fox skins and deer hides were tacked to the walls. A bundle of traps was piled neatly in another corner.

"Name's Pike Moore. Been trappin' wolves up this way for nigh onto fifteen years now.

How come you are up this high?" His matter-of-fact words interrupted Dan's swift inspection.

Pike stirred up the coals in an open fireplace and pulled out a blackened coffeepot. He placed it on the hand-hewn plank table and rummaged around for an extra cup.

Dan cast an oblique look at the big wolfer. "I was trailin' a small jag of stock that drifted this way. Lost their trail in a deep gulch over west of here. I cut back this way to head out and stumbled across that creek. Figured I'd ride up it a ways and check to see if any more of them critters had strayed back into here. When Miss April sent me out to the line shack, she was very positive with orders to check out these draws and back canyons."

"Uh-huh." Pike Moore nodded. He sipped at his scalding coffee, lost in thought.

Dan dug out the makings. He fumbled together a passable cigarette. He pasted it to his upper lip and started to rake a match up his pants leg. His hand stopped, though, when he saw an odd, tense expression in the wolfer's eyes.

Pike Moore's hard face relaxed. A boyish grin tugged at one side of his mouth. His eyes had taken on a shine. They glowed with a dreamlike quality that the younger man could not fathom.

Dan struck the match and lit his cigarette. The glare from the flaming match drew Pike's gaze.

"By golly! Now there is a woman!" The murmur came out low and gentle, completely different from his earlier tone.

Dan's bewilderment mounted. The match burned down to his fingers. He gave a startled yelp and flung it aside. Very carefully, Dan removed the cigarette from his mouth and licked at his burnt fingers.

"You mean Miss April?"

Good gosh, Dan thought, this guy is crazier than a bedbug. Nobody, not even a slab-sided, smelly, tobacco-chewing mule face like Pike Moore, could possibly see April Winters as a likable woman, much less want her.

"Yep. That April is one woman I'd sure like to team up with in double harness," Pike said softly.

Dan strained to hear each low-spoken word. He leaned forward, pressing against the table. His half-numbed brain refused to function correctly. Surely, this weird, semi-hermit living many miles back up here in the wilds couldn't be serious. He had to be pulling Dan's leg. Pulling it hard and twisting it also.

Pike shifted his cud of chewing tobacco and spit into an empty tomato can beside the table. He wiped a grimy sleeve across his whiskery mouth. Then he leaned forward and looked directly at his visitor. The trapper's expression showed that he wanted to unburden his heart, but didn't know exactly where to begin.

Dan gathered in a stray thought and his mind pounced upon it. He remained silent a long moment, letting the glimmer of this strange idea filter through. A mental picture of Pike Moore and April Winters hitched to a plow possessed him, and he grinned in spite of himself.

"Maybe I can help you," Dan mused aloud. But for the life of him, Dan just didn't see exactly how he could.

"I don't know." Pike drained his cup. He turned and reached for the pot.

Dan watched in fascinated awe as Pike's bare hand gripped the pot's hot handle.

Pike didn't seem to feel the heat. He lifted the bubbling pot from the open fire and poured their cups full. He returned the now near-empty pot to the fire, then settled down on his stump. The lines of his horsey face were creased with a deep frown.

"Run across April five, six years ago when I turned in a bunch of wolf and coyote ears. Found out then that she didn't have much use for men."

"So you've just hung around waitin'?" Dan asked. Still, he marveled at the man's interest in April.

"Yep. Managed to talk to her a time or two, but sure didn't seem to get anywhere. She's the toughest female that I've ever seen. Just what a man of my caliber needs." Pike let the last few words trail off and a long silence followed. He gazed into his coffee cup, seemingly lost in deep thought.

Dan felt a glimmer of hope for himself and Spring as that stray idea kept nagging at the back of his mind. Slowly but surely it was developing into a dubious plan.

He raked a thumb over his scratchy chin whiskers and squinted at Pike Moore. "Would you do anything to get Miss April?" Dan asked, trying to keep a wild note of excitement out of his voice.

"Pretty nigh anything, so long as it won't bring the law down on me," Pike asserted.

"I'm not sure if this will work, but I have an idea. You sit tight here. When I get back to the ranch, I'll see what Miss Spring and Miss May think of it. If they agree, I'll get word to you on just what has to be done."

"What do you have in mind?" Pike asked.

"Can't say for sure at the moment. It might not suit the girls. But if it does, and you want to try what I've got in mind, I don't see how it can fail. Trust me. We'll get the details figured out. Might take a few weeks yet before we're ready."

Dan rose to his feet and paced nervously. Pike watched, waiting in a state of suppressed impatience.

Dan caught the look and grinned crookedly. "Stick with me, Pike, and, by golly, we'll whip this yet." Dan pounded a fist into his open palm. "Listen. I best get back down to the line shack. April should be sending a couple of boys up soon to keep an eye on the stock. Soon as they get here, I'll head back to headquarters and get to work."

Dan strode purposefully out the open door, his spurs setting up a cheerful jingle.

"All right," Pike said, but already the rather odd, mild-looking cowboy had vanished from sight. He sat at the rough plank table listening until the jangle of spurs faded and died. Soon he caught the faint fall of hoofbeats. That also quickly faded and a brooding silence fell over the small glade.

Pike Moore sat long at the table. His mind weighed the cowboy's every word. For some time he pondered, wondering what the man had in mind. Surely he, Pike Moore, could not just ride down to the Rafter W and force April to marry him. He had already tried to court her and that had not worked.

His shoulders sagged with a weary resignation. His thoughts turned sour. "Dang," he muttered. "That rider was just blowin' smoke. There ain't nothin' he can do."

The shadows deepened inside the cabin as the high cliff blocked out the lowering sun. They advanced rapidly across the open space until the entire meadow was wreathed in a gloomy darkness that somehow matched Pike Moore's frame of mind.

Pike had no illusions about himself. He was almost forty years old with nothing behind him but a lot of wasted years. Until he found this tiny nook far back in the mountains, he had been content to drift from one range to another.

As a gangling teenager, Pike hunted the last of the great buffalo herds. He scouted for the cavalry and fought against the Sioux of North Dakota. After that he worked as a teamster freighting supplies from St. Louis to Santa Fe. His drifting included a stab at punching cows, but he did not like that.

He trapped in the great Tetons for several seasons before drifting down into Arizona. After a brief visit to Flagstaff, he had outfitted himself with a riding mule and the pack mule that he now had and headed back north. Later, he had come to New Mexico Territory and spotted the small creek. He vividly remembered riding to its head and breaking out into the glade late one evening. He pitched camp and, before the complete darkness closed down around him, Pike could feel a great tranquility within his soul. Here he wanted to stay.

Pike pitched his camp near the bubbling spring. He slept under the stars. The next day he marked out a site for his cabin. A thick stand of the lodgepole pines provided an ample supply of logs.

Soon the cabin took shape. From the cliff facing, he chipped out enough square stones to build the fireplace. A combined pole-and-sod roof completed his sturdy new home.

The cabin was without windows. During warm weather, such as now, Pike kept the door open. In the winter, he merely closed the door, dropping a bar across it to keep it fastened against the blustery winter wind.

Pike finally rose, squaring his sagging shoulders in the cabin's now pitch-black interior. He heaved a mighty sigh. It was a good life, he reflected, lonely as all get-out, but it was good not to be bothered with crowds of people. Always they would be concerned with their petty problems. Sometimes these would be stirred up into bigger troubles by wagging, gossipy tongues.

He reached into the fireplace, knowing unerringly where it was despite the utter darkness. He poked at the now dead ashes, then laid a few pieces of dried pine kindling in their center. A match flared in his hand, causing him to squint against its sudden brightness.

Pike touched the kindling and grunted with satisfaction as it caught fire immediately. He laid two bigger chunks of wood across the tiny flames. Pike stared at the dancing shadows as the fire licked at his fresh fuel. His gnarled hand closed over the cold coffeepot. He stretched leisurely before tramping heavily towards the door on his way to refill the pot with clear, fresh water from his spring.

Chapter Seven

Buck Shedd's high frame formed a dim silhouette by the corral bars at his hidden ranch. He roundly cursed Dutch Otto for a dumb fool.

Tim Alvin cast a furtive look at the raging outlaw leader. But the gathering night hid Shedd's angular features.

Al Hayes slung his saddle over the top rail and muttered, "The dang idiot got shot or something, eh? I thought he might of."

"His horse showed up with broken reins. Might have gotten tangled somewhere. Worse yet, somebody might be able to track him here," Buck said.

"Doubtful," the gnome-sized Hayes reassured his boss. "That ground is pretty rough, and a riderless horse has a tendency to wander. And he's been back for a while now."

"Could be you're right," Shedd said. "We can't take any chances, though. Keep a sharp lookout around here."

A match flared. Shedd drew on a short black cigar. His malevolent eyes glared in the brief light.

A nasty chuckle came from Hayes's dim form. "Nothing good to see, I'll bet."

"Yeah," Shedd snorted. "All these piddling little raids ain't doing much good. Now that Otto got it, the cat's out of the bag."

"You figure it's about time for one big drive?" Hayes asked.

"Past time," Shedd said harshly. He ground the cigar under his heel. "First thing in the morning I'm heading into Raton. You take over here until I get back."

Shedd rode down from the hills early in the morning. He wondered if Ross would go for his idea of a full-scale drive, pronto. No matter, he would pull it off, anyway.

Raton finally hove into sight. Shedd spurred his mount. It responded by breaking into a ground-eating lope.

Also, on this same day, Dan Martin rode back to ranch headquarters. Each mile that brought him closer to home grew longer. He tried hard to put Spring out of his mind.

Chuck Raines and Jack Lester were now at the line shack. They had brought a message from April: Send Dan back so he could work around the home place. Tell him not to wreck anything. Also, she needed him for a trip to town sometime today.

The sun rose higher and warmed the day. Dan shifted in the saddle. He grunted and lightly touched his spurs to the mare's ribs. He pointed her away from an inviting grove of aspens and cut out in a straight line for the ranch.

After a while, he crossed a brushy draw, startling several cows with spring calves. The older animals watched closely as he rode by. One swung her head defiantly when she figured he was too close. Another bellowed out her anger and threatened to charge.

But Dan urged the mare into a brisk canter. A jerk on the lead rope brought the packhorse clattering after. Dan did not have much farther to go.

Finally, he reached the corrals. Then he quickly unbuckled the mare and the packhorse and turned both animals loose in the main enclosure.

His eyes moved towards the big house some distance away. He saw no one. He walked towards the bunkhouse with his bedroll. A longer, closer look still failed to find any signs of anyone at the ranch house.

Dan entered the welcome coolness of the rambling bunkhouse. He tossed his bedroll on an empty bunk and sat down beside it, then pushed his hat back to sleeve sweat from his forehead. With his other hand, he plucked out a nearly empty sack of Bull Durham.

His thoughts drifted idly to the weather while he spun a cigarette. He lit up and puffed silently. His face became wreathed in smoke that slowly rose to drift away.

It was growing hotter each day. Up at the line shack Chuck had started to talk about the forthcoming Fourth of July celebration in town. Plans were being made for horse races, a rodeo, and a huge picnic.

The cowboys were all planning on going into Raton for the celebration. Even Chuck and Jack would come back for fresh supplies in time for the Fourth. Afterwards, they would return to the line shack and continue to work the high country for stray stock.

Further east and south another pair of riders patrolled the Rafter W's boundary. But their job was much easier, for several smaller ranches, one being Adam Brewer's Circle B, lay in that direction.

During the holiday they would also go into town, and the range would be left unguarded.

Dan reviewed this situation and found it an ideal time for the rustlers to strike again. Best stick close and keep an eye peeled, he figured.

Dan felt the quirley burn down to a stub between his fingers. He dropped it to the floor and ground it out with a boot.

A new thought entered his mind. Today's proposed trip to town opened a new door for his investigation. Just might pick up some information about that rustler he had shot.

Buck Shedd strode with long, loose steps towards the Longhorn Saloon. His dark look reflected a sour mood.

The lean outlaw's pace slackened. His gaze swept across the dusty street. It passed over the Rafter W wagon and a lanky cowboy who thumped down a sack of flour atop its load. The cowboy straightened to brush at his shoulder.

Shedd's eyes narrowed. He pushed into the

Longhorn, angling for the bar. The cowboy disturbed him, for there was something vaguely familiar about his looks.

But it was a small thing and Shedd dismissed it from his mind. Hell, there were dozens of riders like that one. Buck had other things to think about.

Ross was getting too high-handed. Once again he had pushed at Shedd about the Rafter W. Ross said he—not Shedd—would decide when the time was right for the big drive.

As Shedd downed a whiskey, the Rafter W rider sauntered into his line of vision.

Dan Martin tipped back his hat. He wiped the sweat from his brow. Sure seemed a lot cooler in the Longhorn.

"Thirsty work loadin' them supplies," he told the bartender. "Give me a beer."

His lazy glance caught Shedd's reflection in the bar mirror. A ruthless thinning of the mouth lingered to denote the lean outlaw's vile dispostion.

Shedd's disturbed thoughts returned. He swung around, half facing the cowboy.

Dan ignored the move as he took a generous swallow of the cool beer. He motioned to the bartender. Now just might be a good time to drop a few hints, he thought. That hombre drinking alone carried the stamp of a surly individual always on the prod.

"Heard tell an old ridin' pard of mine was in these parts," Dan said. "A big man. Dutchman we always called him."

Dan had taken a shot in the dark. He figured that the outlaw he had killed would most likely be tagged Dutch or something close enough to that handle.

"Seems a big fella like that was in a week or two back," the bartender said, flicking at a fly. "Where did you know him?"

"Texas, down Waco way. There were lots of Germans and Dutch settled in there," Dan lied.

"Say!" The bartender glanced at Buck Shedd. "Wasn't that big fella with you and a couple of your boys?"

Shedd's eyes took on a smoldering violence. This waddy knew Dutch but, more than likely, not from Waco.

"Yes. He was lookin' for work, but I didn't hire him," Shedd stated flatly. "And I think you are lying, cowboy. That hombre was from Colorado."

Dan's nerves grew taut. The surly rider had issued a challenge and the response was up to him.

Here was Dan's first real break in the case.

But there was still no solid evidence. A gun battle would accomplish nothing.

Dan quickly studied the man. They were of equal height, although the outlaw might outweigh him by ten pounds.

A smile formed on Dan's face as he unbuckled his gun belt. "Now I just have to take you up on that remark."

Dan put the belt on the bar. Then he slammed a jolting fist into the outlaw's flat stomach.

Shedd grunted and slid away from the bar. One hand flashed for his Colt. But an iron hand clamped down on his wrist. The muscles in his neck corded as Shedd strained against the grip.

He came up chest to chest with the cowboy and swung an awkward left hook. He tried to slam a knee into the cowboy's middle, but a quick shift effectively blocked his move.

Shedd's teeth rattled as Dan ducked and butted his chin. His numbed fingers released the now too heavy Colt. It landed in the thin layer of sawdust and slid away to lodge against a chair.

Suddenly, the grip loosened on Shedd's wrist. Another solid blow slammed into his ribs. A hard right cross rocked his jaw. Shedd staggered backwards and smashed into a table.

Dan pressed his advantage. He knew that this man was a gunman and disdained fist fighting. But it didn't pay to take any chances now. For back in Shedd's past, he just might have been in several rough-and-tumble fights. Dan did not intend to learn the hard way.

Shedd cursed and spat out a thin stream of blood. His malevolent eyes searched wildly for his Colt. He saw it a few feet away and dived, trying to kick a chair into the charging cowboy's path.

Dan brushed the chair aside. His lunging boot caught Shedd's forearm. The Colt spun away.

A strong grasp pulled Shedd to his feet. He essayed a feeble kick that slid off Dan's shin. Two quick, rock-hard blows drummed at his aching ribs.

Shedd doubled over with a grunt of pain. Dan straightened him with a left to the jaw. As Shedd came up, a chopping right smashed into his chin.

Dan stepped aside as the outlaw swayed and fell face down. He stared at the limp form for a moment, then spun back to lean over the bar. His breath came short and quick for several seconds.

A warning came from the bartender. "You best be careful now. He'll shoot on sight next time you cross his path."

Dan buckled on his gun belt. He massaged a swelling knuckle. "Reckon so," he replied tersely.

And, he thought, the rustlers would be mad and not quite so cautious. Business would surely pick up!

Chapter Eight

The wagon bounced over a rocky stretch of road. Dan felt as if his insides would be jarred loose.

He flipped the lines. This encouraged the team to pull harder up a slanting rise.

The fight with Shedd, he figured, should stir that hombre into some kind of action. But just when would he make his strike?

Dan realized that the odds of catching Shedd in the act were still very much against him. The rustlers would somehow have to be flushed into the open. Just maybe this day's work would help.

Marshal McCoy was no great help, though. He had no reason to pick up Shedd. And he chose to ignore the fight, saying that the two men had settled their differences.

It still seemed likely that the rustlers would strike while most everyone was in town for the Fourth. As a mere cowhand—and a pretty new one at that—Dan was in no position to tell anyone that they should keep some armed men with the herd on the Fourth. But he could keep his eyes and ears free of dust.

Another thought kept bothering him, though. Was Shedd the main leader? It just did not add up for Dan. A hunch told him no.

But how to catch the big boss, if there was one? This job was stacking up to be a little harder than usual. And there was much more distraction, also. Dan mulled over the problems that he had encountered.

"Reckon this will be my last job for Cap Franklin," he mused aloud. "That is, if things work out like I hope. Reckon there is no great future to throwin' guns and chasin' bad guys. May just see about a little spread around here. I kinda like this country."

Long shadows etched their way across the trail. Tall pines swayed in an evening breeze.

Dan said to the team, "Giddy up there. Quit laggin' or you'll be late for the feedbag tonight."

The horses strained at their collars. The

wagon jolted over a rock. Dan slid sideways on the high-backed seat.

Just then something tugged at his sleeve, and the thin sound of a rifle broke into his thoughts.

Dan never stopped moving. He dropped the lines and dived headlong off the wagon, rolling into a small depression. Another rifle shot was heard.

The team was spooked. They began a clumsy run. The wagon rattled across a small stream.

Dan felt for his pistol. A wave of relief washed over him as he gripped the Colt's handle.

Now who could that be? he wondered. Was Shedd mad enough to ambush him?

Dan cautiously peered over the lip of ground. He swept the dim trees ahead, searching for the rifleman.

But he could see nothing among the shadows. Dan knew that he could not stay here.

Not far from him, a screen of brush bordered the mountain stream. Just beyond this grew a scattering of squat sycamore trees.

He was nearing the brush when the rifle cracked again. It sounded from higher up this time.

The whining slug whipped by his ear. He dived into the brush.

Dan worked his way through the brush until he could make a run for a rather large sycamore.

It was growing darker, and the fickle wind shifted. It carried the sound of faintly drumming hoofbeats.

Dan listened carefully. This wasn't the team. They had stopped after only a short run. No, that had to be the bushwhacker hightailing it out of the country.

Dan looked at his torn sleeve. Now that was a close shave. Just about as close as he had ever come.

He holstered the big Colt. This job was beginning to heat up.

The rustlers would strike for sure now, Dan figured. They had become bold enough to try an ambush. Things should be popping soon.

Buck Shedd sheathed his still-warm rifle. He mounted a tall bay. His spurs rammed viciously into the horse's flanks.

Damn the luck, he thought. That cowpuncher had all of it. That wagon would have to jolt just as he drew a fine bead on his target.

Another split second and he would have drilled that waddy dead center.

Shedd squinted through his right eye. The left eye was swollen shut. A purple lump blended with dark whisker stubble on his jaw. His bruised ribs protested each time the bay put a hoof down.

Shedd wondered, though. That cowboy sure did flop when he went into the brush. Maybe he should have checked the place. He might have nailed him good. Anyway, he hoped so.

He dipped into a sandy gully that led to his hidden ranch. The bay slowed. His hooves made a soft, swishing sound in the sand.

Suddenly, Shedd sat up straight in the saddle. He grunted with a knifing pain. One hand pressed at his hurt ribs.

Now he remembered. That was no ordinary cowboy, but one of Franklin's range detectives.

Deming, wasn't it, where he had seen the man? Sure, Shedd was positive now. It would be best to lay low until the Fourth drew everybody into Raton.

The big front door to the barn was repaired and rehung. Dan saw April swing into the saddle and charge out of the yard at a high lope. Soon afterwards Spring hurried across the yard.

They sat side by side on a pile of loose hay Dan finally broke the silence. "Listen, Spring, I got an idea. Do you know Pike Moore?"

"Why, yes, I've seen him in town a time or two, and he came by here once." Spring looked sideways at Dan. "Oh, no! Are you thinking of him for April?"

"Sure am. Ran across him maybe ten miles back up in the hills behind that northwest line shack. He's quite a character. Told me he's in love with April and will do nearly anything to get her."

Spring burst into a gale of laughter. "Oh, that would be really swell, but how?"

"Here's my idea," Dan said. "The day before the Fourth, have May kinda drop a hint that she is riding over to see this Adam Brewer. I know she likes him. Do you think April will follow her?"

"Yes. I know she will." Spring appeared slightly puzzled. "But what if she doesn't?"

"Hint that you think they're running off to get married," Dan suggested.

"Ah," Spring said softly. "That would do it."

"Good. I'll get May to relay a message through Brewer to Pike. He's to come down and stay with Brewer. Pike can hide out near where May and Adam meet. Here's the touchy part. Pike might not go for it, but I think he will.

"He'll have to waylay April. Trap her, rope her, or however he wants to catch her. Then carry her off to that cabin of his back in the hills. I don't think anybody knows exactly where it is but me. I'll pass those directions on to Brewer."

"But that's kidnapping, not getting married," Spring cried.

"I figure it this way," Dan said. "April needs to be broke just like a wild mustang. Old Pike can kinda put a halter on her and gentle her down for a few days. Then she'll come around."

"What happens, though, if April doesn't want to be broke, as you say? She could get away or Pike Moore just might turn her loose if she puts up too strong a fight," Spring worried.

"Well, I think there's nothing to lose," Dan said. "It's our only chance. Nobody around here wants her and she for darn sure don't want any of them, either. Now Pike impressed me as quite an hombre. And the thing is, he actually loves April, believe it or not. I think they'll get along fine. You know, April has never given any man a chance before. Pike is rougher around the edges than she is. Probably just what she needs."

"Okay! We'll do it!" Spring agreed. Excitement brightened her eyes. She could scarcely hold back a wild laughter that welled up in her breast. Her entire being quivered.

"That a girl!" Dan said.

After Spring vanished out the barn's rear entrance, he lounged back on the pile of hay. He idly picked at the loose straw, placing a long stem in his mouth and chewing on it.

He told himself he was working on everything except the job that he had been sent to do.

The next week or so was uneventful. Dan managed to see Spring several times. She assured him that the plans were being put into motion.

May was more than agreeable. Adam Brewer, after a hard search, had located Pike Moore. According to Brewer's report, the mountain man had taken to the plan with alacrity.

Now it was only a matter of setting up April. That would be the easiest part, though.

Old Howlin' Winters, who had been visiting the ranch, had hitched up his buggy a few days before and ridden off. So he was out of the way and could not interfere with their scheme.

Chuck Raines and Jack Lester rode in late one night reporting that all was well near their line shack. More outriders drifted in also, filling the bunkhouse with their boisterous laughter. It was their release of pent-up emotions after being stationed in the lonely line shacks.

They bragged endlessly about their horses and each one bet the other that he would win the best-all-around-cowboy award at the forthcoming rodeo. Riding gear was repaired and polished.

April found a few loose boards on the front veranda. She ordered Dan to fix them. Then she said, "On the Fourth I want someone to stay on the place. We can't leave it completely deserted. Since you are the newest hand, you can stay home and take care of the chores."

While Dan was fixing the veranda, June came over. They quickly exchanged greetings.

Then she said, "Tell Jack not to try and see

me until the Fourth. Then he should meet me after the third dance. He'll know what I mean." June's words trailed off into silence.

Dan pounded industriously on the final nail before rising and brushing off his pants. He stepped hurriedly off the veranda as heavy footsteps sounded just inside the house.

Dan could hear the front door squeak open and then slam shut as he walked with rapid strides towards the toolshed. He flinched, expecting to hear April's harsh tones. But the silence held and he gradually slowed his pace.

A low whistle split Dan's lips. He couldn't carry a tune in a tow sack and didn't care. His keyed-up nerves needed some form of release.

He entered the stifling little shed. The heat didn't bother him, either. He put the hammer away and sat down on a handy nail keg.

Well, what a surprise, Dan mused. That June sure turned out to be one surprising woman. So she wants Jack to meet her at the dance. Sure hope they want to get hitched. With April, May, and June out of the way, me and Spring will have a clear shot at it ourselves. April's the only big problem. Don't let me down now, Pike Moore!

The bell for supper interrupted his musing.

Dan hurried to wash up. He trooped into the cook shack and jostled for a place at the table.

And what a meal. Fong had outdone himself.

The table swayed and groaned under heaping platters of steak. There was an abundance of fried potatoes and gravy. Somewhere along the line, Fong had learned to make light bread. Now he placed several loaves before the cheerfully hungry men.

Fong told the men to eat well today and tomorrow. For he would then be taking a few days off to celebrate the Fourth.

After the meal, Dan sauntered outside. He strolled to the main corral and leaned against a peeled pole as he rolled a quirley. He wondered how things would work out tomorrow and the next day.

Chapter Nine

April was up and about, and more energetic than usual. She inspected the barn and corrals.

The place seemed to be in good shape. But something continued to nag her. Maybe it was that squeaky windmill, she thought.

Despite her outwardly dour look, April felt a keening excitement over the festivities in Raton the day after tomorrow. She tramped towards the big house.

The sun hung overhead, seemingly suspended in the sky. Heat waves shimmered across the yard.

April paused near the veranda. She turned to survey the surrounding hills and something caught her eye. Rising bits of dust. She squinted through the bright sunlight.

Now who can that be? she wondered. Sure wasn't expecting anybody to come from town.

April waited out the minutes. Slowly the lifting dust grew closer. She made out a high-stepping white horse pulling a shiny town buggy.

Her brows knitted together. The corpulent shape took form. A pudgy hand lifted in a half wave.

April snorted in disbelief. Now what was that fat toad, Ross, doing out here? It sure wasn't any social call.

The buggy spun to a stop. Dust settled over its top. More dust drifted away on a lazy breeze.

The white horse blew. His head tossed. He was eager to head for the water trough.

Ross checked the animal. "Good morning, Miss Winters." He held up a hand. "No, don't bother to invite me in. I only have a moment."

He produced a fat envelope from his vest pocket. "Do you know what this is?" he asked.

"How in thunderation do I know?" April replied crossly. What was the fat merchant up to now? she silently asked herself.

"I have here," Ross said rather pompously, "many chits for supplies charged at my store.

Too many, in fact. They must be paid."

He continued before April could reply. "Also, you realize that I now own a controlling interest in the bank." Ross smiled smugly at this statement.

"So what?" April asked. "That ain't none of my affair."

"Oh? But it is," Ross said. His tone grew demanding. "The mortgage to this place is also here. And it's way past due. As noted in these papers, you are to make a payment each spring and fall. No payment has been made this year."

"You'll get your money," April said testily. "Soon as fall roundup and shipping is done, I'll pay all the notes off."

"Ah, but that's not the way it works," Ross purred. "I have here a court order. You have thirty days to pay up or I take over, lock, stock, and barrel."

"You can't do that," April raged. "Why, we built this ranch. There never has been any question before about payment."

"That was then. This is now. Times change." Ross let his voice harden even more. "There will be no more credit at the store." He spun the buggy around and drove away at a smart clip.

April stood rooted in her tracks. Dust showered her still form. She brushed angrily at the annoying film.

Where did that blithering idiot get off thinking he could take over the Rafter W? she fumed.

There was plenty of stock on the range for a quick gather. Although it would mean taking a beating on prices, she didn't get concerned about the money.

It was Ross's high-handed attitude that got her dander up. Cut off her credit, would he? By golly, she would show him. After she paid the notes, the Rafter W would buy somewhere else. It might mean a longer haul, but Ross would soon learn the error of his ways. Why, without their ranch, he might as well lock his store.

April ground out a silent curse. Her boots resounded as she strode purposefully across the veranda.

Stanley Ross knew an inner satisfaction as he rode away from the ranch. His ultimatum would give that homely redhead plenty to think about.

His mouth split into a leering smile. Shedd was demanding action. The time was right.

Let Shedd drive off all the stock that could be mustered. Scatter the rest. Then April Winters would not have enough cows to raise the needed money.

Ross's small eyes smoked. June would be in town the next day for sure. Soon he could approach her with his proposal.

The road wound into a rather deep gully. He crossed its mouth. The white horse labored up to the far side.

Ross topped the steep hill. He reined in under a spreading sycamore. His pig eyes shifted nervously.

This had to be the place, he thought. The steep hill and spreading tree matched Shedd's description.

He fumbled in a vest pocket and pulled out a fine silver watch. It was after ten. He shifted with irritation. The buggy seat was becoming too hard for his backside.

The time was right, just as Shedd had agreed, but where was the blasted rustler? Ross waited until his temper reached the boiling point. Finally, he prepared to leave.

"Hold up, Ross." The harsh voice came from just behind him. Shedd soon moved alongside the buggy.

"You're late," Ross complained. He frowned sternly.

"Cut out the lectures," Shedd warned. "I waited to make sure nobody followed you."

"I'll bet," Ross said. "Anyway, what did you want to see me about?"

"No time for this small talk," Shedd replied. "Are you ready for the big push now?"

"Yes! The sooner, the better." Excitement made Ross's voice a notch higher than usual. "Hit them hard. I want that Winters bunch on their knees."

Shedd's face twisted into the semblance of a smile. They discussed the Rafter W. Then Shedd said, "You just drive on back to Raton and leave this end to me."

Ross said, "Horses coming. You scoot. I'll be in touch after the drive."

Shedd vanished behind the buggy. He ran down a narrow draw to where his mount was tied. Moments later he was in the saddle.

But he waited, holding in the bay. He heard Ross's buggy rattle off down the road. Not long after, a pair of bantering cowboys thundered down the road.

Shedd let an evil grin show. He turned the bay southward and put the animal into a gallop. He had thinking to do. Might as well take a nice long ride.

Night shrouded the land before Shedd reached his ranch. Somewhere in the dark, an owl hooted. Shedd's bay whickered, anxious to enter the corral and be with his companions.

Shedd let the bay have his head. Not far from the corral, he reined in, though, and dismounted. The bay eased off, reins trailing.

A rectangle of yellow splashed across the yard. Shedd studied the open door. He could hear laughter coming from inside the house.

His long stride quickly placed him squarely in the light. He stepped inside and kicked the door shut.

Bud Stone froze. He had been about to lay down his poker hand and claim a big pot.

Tim Alvin leaped up, startled. His clawing hand stopped in midair as he recognized Shedd.

Al Hayes came from a back room. He looked sleepily at Shedd.

"What the hell is going on here?" Shedd demanded. "Why ain't there any guard posted?"

Hayes snapped, "Bud, get out there and see

where that dang kid, Vernell, is. He's supposed to be on guard."

"Bud, when you find him, you two slope back here," Shedd added.

"What's up, boss?" Alvin asked.

Shedd waved the question aside. His eyes ranged around the room. They finally settled on a pair of seedy-looking, middle-aged riders.

"We'll move tomorrow. Jim, you and Whiskey Zack hit over on the east ranges in the day. Pick up what stock you can handle in a hurry. Scatter the rest."

His brooding eyes centered on Vernell as the kid stepped inside the room. "The rest of us will cut through the heart of the Rafter W. The time is ripe. Tomorrow night!"

Chapter Ten

April Winters made one last inspection of the ranch before heading for the house. She stopped by the corrals to see if Dan—with the two left feet and hands—was carrying out her orders.

The rush of hoofbeats broke the quiet morning. April pulled up short with a quick, "Oh, darn! There goes May to meet that darn Brewer like she said she would." Ross was completely forgotten.

April spun and headed for the main corral. She caught up her mount where it stood tied, saddled, and ready. A fast leap put her into the hull. The hard thrust of spurs pushed her mount into a dead run. It flashed around the

barn and disappeared in the general direction
of Turkey Creek.

Dan waited until the dust settled. He then
headed for the bunkhouse.

The crew thundered out of the yard. He
thought they made a mighty grand sight
heading into Raton and the big celebration
coming up the next day.

Slowly the boiling dust cloud drifted and
settled. Dan stirred, then stopped short.

Spring Winters and her three remaining
sisters emerged from the ranch house. They
climbed into a shiny, high-topped buggy that
was ready and waiting.

Spring spun the patient old gray buggy horse
around. She flicked the lines, clucked to the
animal, and they were also off to town.

Dan stood stock-still. He alone remained on
the ranch, for even Fong had departed for town
with the crew. Several lagging minutes ticked
away. Finally, he moved, walking rapidly into
the bunkhouse.

It was a marvelous jumble of disorder. The
smell of stale sweat fought against strong odors
of cheap hair tonic and whiskey. Cigarette
smoke still lingered in the corners and near
the low ceiling.

Dan kicked aside a tangle of unwashed

clothing. He pushed a pair of scarred chaps out of his way as he headed towards his bunk. He reached for the makings and spun a quirley, finishing off the near empty sack.

Then Dan dug a clean change of clothes out of his warbag. They were somewhat worn and wrinkled but serviceable. He dressed quickly before searching out a fresh sack of Bull and thin sheaf of papers.

Dan lay down on his bunk. He rolled another quirley, moodily contemplating the day ahead of him. He smoked in deep silence, wavering between dark thoughts. He felt helpless. Should he pack and leave? Just shuck this whole rustler business? He knew about Buck Shedd, but he didn't have a shred of real evidence against the man.

He expelled a long, thin stream of smoke. He watched it grow even thinner as it wafted upwards.

The quirley burned down. He flipped it into a butt-can. It fizzled and went out.

Dan reflected on his next move. The rustlers could strike anywhere. And he could only be one place at a time.

Might as well track April for a while, he finally decided. He at least owed Spring that much. And at the same time he could watch the range for any signs of a drive. If he found none, then he would head on to Santa Fe and make his report.

Dan strapped on his gun belt and slung the bedroll over his shoulder. He would see how things were working out with May and her man. There was a darn good chance that Pike Moore might not be able to handle April.

If not, he figured to head into town and warn Spring before he headed out to the country. For April would be on the warpath, madder than a stirred-up hornets' nest.

Dan roped his sorrel gelding out of the corral and saddled it. He cast one long, last look around the deserted ranch after he got into the saddle. A light touch of the spurs put his sorrel into motion.

An ungovernable rage possessed April this day. Why, darn it, did May have to pick today to elope with that shirttail rancher on Turkey Creek? Funny thing, April thought, May had never openly rebelled before or really said much one way or the other about them marrying in order of their ages.

Marriage! April thought irately. Men! Bah. She didn't need them. At no time in her life could she remember one that interested her.

But a seed of doubt crept into her mind. The picture came to her of a tall, slab-sided wolfer who had visited the ranch. She couldn't remember much about him other than that he was rough and bearded. Now, as then, a strange twinge ran up her spine.

"Aw, heck, that was ages ago, and I never did know his name," she muttered.

April slashed her quirt across the laboring horse's rump. Her cruel spurs bit into the bay.

The horse raced onward at a faster pace. But April couldn't gain any ground on May. April followed, now and then losing sight of her quarry as she dipped over the low hills. This didn't bother April, though, for a plume of trailing dust marked May's passage.

April grunted. She had to give May credit for choosing a good horse. Fleeting glimpses had shown April that May was riding a big, deep-chested black. And the black was equal in speed to her own bay. April finally became concerned, for her own mount was beginning to break. It just might be that the black would outlast him.

Once again May crested a small but steep hill and disappeared down its backside. April reached the hill shortly. She urged her straining, foam-flecked steed up the slope.

He slipped once, almost going down, but April's strong arm on the reins pulled his head up. The lashing quirt pushed him to the top.

April pulled up with a start. There lay Turkey Creek. It wasn't much of a stream this time of year. But thick brush and spreading willows marked its meandering southward direction. Below and slightly to her right Turkey Creek suddenly made a sharp bend as it turned due south.

May had completely vanished. April swept the creek's line in both directions. Still no sign of May.

The bay stood, head hanging and flanks heaving. He slobbered for breath, gave a great heave, and blew a thin spray of foam from his nostrils. April leaned forward in the saddle and patted his hot sweat-lathered shoulder.

Her ranging survey picked out a darker shadow in the sharp bend of Turkey Creek. Her eyes narrowed as they centered on this object.

Surprisingly, it moved. May broke into the open, now on the other side of the willows. She shaded her eyes, casting anxious looks to the east, as if her man was late arriving to meet her.

May looked ahead for several seconds before

craning around in the saddle to look behind her. April was clearly skylined atop the hill. May's shoulders seemed to slump in despair when she saw the waiting figure.

April gave a derisive snort. Just like a fool man! You could not depend on one for anything. She gigged the blowing bay into a slow trot as she angled down the hill heading for the bend in Turkey Creek. Again she snorted, for May seemed to huddle lower in the saddle, giving it all up for a lost cause.

Now only Turkey Creek separated her from May. April fully intended to give her sister a good dressing down and a taste of the quirt. Her earlier rage boiled forth.

April forced the tired bay through a tangle of brush. Bullheaded, obstinate as ever, she never allowed herself to think that May was bait for a trap. She broke free of the brush.

A long shadowy form blended with the closely spaced willows. April could see her sister still sitting quietly, head down, and looking chastised as she waited.

The shadowy form moved. A man stepped out behind April. His arm moved slightly. A loud hiss passed her ears. Suddenly, the thrown rope coiled around April's body, pinning her arms to her sides.

It never occurred to April that she should cry out for help. Instead, she slapped home the spurs.

But that was a great mistake. Pike Moore dug in his heels. Her horse's sudden lunge against the already taut rope separated April from the saddle. She sprawled backwards over the bay's rump to land with a crashing thud.

The breath whooshed from her lungs. Small stones gouged at her back. A broken stick thrust against one hip.

April moved about and tried to stand, but a swift jerk on the rope kept her down. She glared back over one shoulder. A tall, bearded man dressed in greasy buckskins approached. He kept the rope tight, as if holding a calf to the ground ready for branding.

Across the creek a merry laugh sounded. It was joined by a loud whoop. The whoop tailed off to be followed by the receding sounds of rapid hoofbeats.

April was furious. She burned bright red, then turned pale, so great was her anger. She glared balefully at her captor.

Somehow, he seemed awfully tall and strong as he loomed over her. She fought back a rare thrill as he stood quietly regarding her.

Suddenly, Pike allowed the rope to loosen.

But before April could wiggle free, he planted an overlarge moccasined foot smack dab in the middle of her stomach.

Pike Moore rolled his cud of tobacco from one cheek to the other. He chewed thoughtfully for a moment, then turned his head briefly and spit.

"Well, now, honey," Pike drawled. There was no trace of gentleness in his harsh tones. A calculating look centered on April's pale, freckle-studded face. "Will you promise to be a good girl and come along nice and easy if I let you up? I just want us to talk some, get acquainted."

"Go to Hades!" April gasped hoarsely. She was still very much incensed over her ignoble position.

Now she knew who he was, for she suddenly remembered the name, Pike Moore. She tried to glare hatefully and couldn't. Her baleful green eyes were only half as fiery as usual. But then she got angrier. Sort of.

The man's easy capture of her added fuel to April's fury. But for some unknown reason she caught herself turning all the anger inward.

April blinked. His heel dug into the pit of her stomach. Still, she only seethed at her own feelings. She turned her head away, afraid to look at the man's cool gaze, for fear that he might discover her unsettled feelings. She slowly relaxed.

"If that's the way you want it," Pike Moore said, "reckon I'll just have to hobble you and put a curb bit in your mouth. I'll break you like a wild mustang."

April barely heard the last words for he seemed to be talking to himself.

April felt the rope's pressure relent slightly. She sprang erect, whirling to face Pike. Her mouth opened to curse him. But it snapped shut with a loud click. For Pike Moore cuffed the side of her head with a rough palm.

Pain flooded her ear. She flew backwards, tripped, and sprawled full length in the dirt, unable to move. But she could feel his big, strong hands draw hers together. Swift, and none too gentle, he bound them wrist to wrist. She felt a hard twist around her ankles and added pain. He lifted her up.

Then her head hung down his back. She watched the ground, ignominiously draped over his shoulder.

He stopped suddenly. A quick heave and she flopped belly-down over her saddle.

April hung limp, weak, and spent as all the breath was forced from her lungs. She gasped for air, unable to damn him while he expertly tied her to the saddle.

Pike said, "Anytime you get tired of riding belly-down, just holler. All you have to do is promise to cooperate, to talk to me nicely."

April took in his expressionless eyes. "You-can-go-to-Hades," she managed to gasp.

"That's all right with me." Pike Moore shrugged.

He loosened his grip. April was not prepared for the sudden release. Her head flopped and her nose banged against the saddle skirt.

The pain made her eyes watery. She tried to heap curses upon him, but the sudden motion of the horse cut her off short.

Chapter Eleven

May Winters rode stirrup to stirrup with Adam Brewer. Her hat flew back to hang by its chin strap. Her short brown hair ruffled in the wind.

She knew, for the first time, a complete feeling of freedom. Nothing, May reflected, could spoil her utter happiness.

The Circle B lay before them. Although it was not nearly so large as the Rafter W, Adam Brewer ran a neat, prosperous ranch. May's heart swelled with pride. Soon she would be mistress over the trim main house at this ranch. She could hardly wait to see the inside of her soon-to-be new home.

Adam Brewer reined his sturdy black Morgan to a stop in front of the house. He stepped heavily out of his stock saddle and reached up to help May dismount.

His round face beamed. May marveled at his strength as he easily lifted her to the ground. May smiled up at her big, burly husband-to-be. Gosh, he sure is big, she thought for the thousandth time.

For Adam Brewer towered well over six feet tall and weighed about two hundred and fifty pounds. When he walked into a room, his very size caused heads to turn and conversation to hush. Some even swore that the building shook under his heavy strides. It took a really strong horse to carry him very far.

"Hey, boss!" someone shouted across the serene ranch yard.

Both turned to look towards the bunkhouse.

One of Brewer's hired hands hurried to intercept them. May vaguely recalled the small, middle-aged stringy man known only as Jasper.

A chew of tobacco bulged in one cheek. His long, drooping mustache twitched as he methodically worked on his chew. It seemed to match his pale, washed-out brown eyes, giving him a melancholy appearance.

Jasper's awkward strides brought him up with a breathless rush. His thin shoulders hunched. "Bad news, boss," he panted.

Adam's round face lost its cherublike look. His heavy eyebrows knitted together. "What is it, Jasper?" he asked.

The cowhand drew a deep breath. "We got trouble. Me and the kid were up to the north pasture when a bunch of salty characters jumped up. We cut and run, but they plugged the kid in the back. I got him to the bunk-house, but ain't too sure if he'll make it. He lost a lot of blood."

A blank look crossed Adam Brewer's genial countenance as the shock of this statement sank home. "Rustlers?" he finally managed.

Jasper turned and spat. "Could be, boss. We had a small jag of blooded Herefords up there. They might have been after them, but we sure didn't stick around to find out."

Adam shook his head, puzzled. "Why here, now?" he groaned. "May, this sure spoils it for us today. Will you take care of the boy?" At her quick nod of assurance, he motioned to Jasper.

"Fog up the dust for town. Bring the doc back soon as you can. I'm going after those cow thieves!"

"Adam, not by yourself?" May placed a hand on his thick forearm.

"Don't worry. I can take care of myself," he reassured her. "Jasper, see if you can round up a posse and follow the trail."

The cowhand shook his head. "Might be kind of hard to scare up anybody, what with the celebration and rodeo goin' on." He heeled around. "I'll sure give it a try, though."

May swiftly kissed Adam, then hurried to the bunkhouse. There she found the young cowhand, Wesley Tyler, awake and alert.

He stirred weakly and tried a wan smile. Startling bright blue eyes stared up mutely as May placed a hand on his damp forehead.

"Not much fever yet," she murmured. "Be still now," May ordered when the youthful cowboy tried to move. "I'm going to clean your wound and pack on a fresh bandage."

"Yes, ma'am," Tyler said softly. "Who are you?"

"Hush, child. I'm soon to be Mrs. Brewer. But first let's see what can be done for you. No, don't move. We don't want that wound to start bleeding again."

May worked with deft hands. She finished and tucked a blanket around the boy's slim figure.

May stepped back and noted that he now slept quietly. She heaved a deep sigh and sat down near the bed. She could hear his shallow breath coming slow, but regular, and knew that this was a good sign.

Her eyes shuttled to an open window, but the cloud of dust that had marked her man's departure had long since settled back to earth.

May waited patiently by the young cowboy's bed. She worried as the fever built, hoping that the doctor would be able to come when Jasper reached him.

She studied the youth's haggard features and found that he was not a bad-looking young man. Just the shadow of a beginning beard blurred his firm jawline.

Dark hair, that was sadly in need of a trim, curled around his ears. May caught herself thinking that as soon as he could sit up, she would give it a good whacking off.

But for Tyler the worst was yet to come. His fever rose. May waited out the long hours. She worried over the injured youth and worried about Adam, wondering where he was.

The sun lowered and still there was no sign of improvement in Tyler's condition. May checked the road to town, but knew in so doing that it was still too soon to expect Jasper to return with the doctor.

Several minutes, fraught with suspense, passed as Tyler sank lower in his feverish condition. May rested for a moment.

The rapid drumming of hoofbeats broke into her deep concentration. She moved slowly to the bunkhouse door and peered out.

At first she failed to recognize the slender rider. But as the fast-racing animal emerged from a shadow on the trail, May let out a tiny gasp. "Autumn." She waved and the rider veered towards the bunkhouse.

Autumn pulled up her lathered steed and dismounted with a flourish. "Hi, May!" An impish devil danced in the girl's eyes.

"You sure raised the devil and put a chunk under him," Autumn laughed. Her smile faded and she quickly sobered under May's stern stare.

But May couldn't stay mad at this sweet, although peevish, little sister that she still thought of as a small child. A glad light of welcome warmed her frowning face. "What are you doing here?" she asked.

"Oh, I ran into that cowhand of Adam's. Jasper. He told me to give you a message. The doctor is off down at that nester family on Little Turkey Creek delivering another baby. Jasper's riding down there to see if he can get the doctor to hurry back here as soon as he can."

"Oh, no," May groaned. Her shoulders heaved with a huge sigh. "Come on in, Autumn. You'll have to help me sit up with the boy. He's in pretty bad shape."

An afterthought suddenly came to her. "What did you mean by that remark about raising the devil?"

Autumn tossed her hat and gloves onto an empty bunk. She shook out her shining blond hair. "June ran off with that bronc-buster, Jack Lester. Nobody knows where they are right now. And Summer was with Chuck Raines looking for the parson. April hasn't shown up in town yet. Boy, will Pa be mad when he hears about all this." She moved to stand over Wesley Tyler's bed.

Suddenly he reached out and clasped her hand in a surprisingly strong grip. His eyes were wide and staring.

"Gosh," he said. "I must have died and gone to heaven, for you sure are a vision."

Autumn nearly fainted as she studied the

cowboy's pallid features. A strangely tender smile formed on her lips.

"No, you haven't died yet, cowboy. And I'm not going to let you die now."

Chapter Twelve

Buck Shedd rode cautiously. One hand rested on the worn butt of his six-shooter. Not far behind him Shedd could hear horns clacking together. And an occasional lowing drifted up the canyon as the tired cattle shuffled along. They kept moving, driven by the relentless riders at their heels.

But they would not go much further, Shedd thought with a nagging worry. Where was Al Hayes?

Shedd's mount stumbled, almost done in by the rough, hard riding that the outlaw demanded that night. Shedd fumed. He yanked the slobbering bay's head up.

They had better reach Hayes and the fresh mounts soon. Or somebody would be walking. And it would not be him.

The canyon suddenly widened into a small, oval-shaped bowl. Shedd snarled with satisfaction as he made out the bunched shapes of many horses.

Al Hayes rode out of the gloom. His gnome-like body made a dark lump in the saddle. "Looks like you made a good gather," he commented as the mixed herd streamed past.

"Yeah," Shedd grunted testily. "Carl, ease up on the herd. We'll rest here till daylight," he called out as Tucker rode slowly in, pushing the last of the drags.

"Gotcha, boss." Tucker sounded worn-out. But he spurred his flagging gelding into a clumsy lope along the herd's flank. "Hold up, boys. Let 'em belly up at the creek. Boss says we're stoppin' here."

Hayes kindled a cheery campfire and put a pot of water on to boil. When he judged it to be hot enough, Hayes tossed in some coffee grounds.

He watched the water simmer and roil for several minutes before sliding the pot away from the flames. Slowly the grounds settled until only a few floated on top of the bitter black brew.

Buck Shedd waited impatiently for his men to ride in. They grouped around the fire, each nursing a cup of Hayes's potent brew. Bud Stone produced a bottle of whiskey and laced his coffee liberally.

"Hey. Gimme some of that," Tim Alvin said, perking up at the sight of the amber liquid.

"Yeah. Me, too," Carl Tucker said.

"Go easy on that swill," Shedd ordered harshly. He strode over to Bud and laced his cup with a small dab of the raw-smelling whiskey.

Carl Tucker sprawled heavily just outside the flickering light. "What now, Buck?" he asked.

Shedd stared dourly into the flames. Something just did not stack up right to the wily outlaw. This deal of Ross's seemed too pat.

When asked about a half interest in the Rafter W, Ross had given in awfully easy. Now just what did he have up his sleeve? Shedd worried the thought like a dog with a bone.

Could this be a sellout? Might be Ross had slipped word somehow to the rangers and they were waiting in Durango.

Shedd rubbed his neck. The last thing he wanted was a noose and a fidgety horse. A shudder crept involuntarily up his lean frame.

"Are we pullin' out of this neck of the woods after this job?" Alvin's question jarred him back to the problem at hand. What to do about Ross?

"Tell you boys what," Shedd replied slowly. "I have a deal with Stanley Ross for a piece of this range. You all push on in the morning and sell this bunch. You can either split up the money between you and drift, or you can head on back to Raton and tie up with me in this deal. Either way, we all stand to come out sittin' pretty." He watched their faces closely while the words sank in.

A skeptical frown pinched Tucker's brows together. Bud Stone shook his head, his mind already made up to move on. Greed brightened Tim Alvin's already glossy eyes.

Only Al Hayes seemed to consider the long-range implications of Shedd's offer. He remained quiet, thinking it out while the others argued amongst themselves.

Finally, he spoke, the words so low that Shedd had to strain to hear him. "You just might see me back in a few days. I'm mighty tired of night ridin'. Anyways, I always figured there was more to this deal than just a little rustlin' operation. Old Baldy Ross has his plans, huh? Now who in town would think it?"

Shedd tossed away the last dregs of the bitter coffee. He called, "Vernell!" And when he had gained the man's attention he ordered, "Swap my saddle over to a fresh animal. I'm goin' to head for Raton and make sure that Ross don't botch this deal."

Tom Vernell, the youngest member of the gang, rose and stepped away from the fire. A sullen scowl creased the gangling youth's brow.

"I ain't your fetch-and-carry boy, Shedd. Change your own saddle." His defiant words ended in a high squeak. His hands spread clawlike over twin Colts that rode low on his hips.

Buck Shedd cast a piercing gaze on Vernell. He waited out the tense moments, not speaking.

Slowly, but surely, Vernell's resolve broke under the outlaw chieftain's hard stare. Sweat beaded his fuzzy cheeks. It trickled down his back and suddenly he wilted. "All right," Vernell muttered. He spun and stalked away into the night.

"Best move back out of the light, Buck. That boy's just been shamed. And he's not playing with a full deck, either. Somebody's goin' to plug him and soon if I don't miss my guess."

This advice came from Al Hayes.

But the words of warning were not necessary. Shedd melted behind the sheltering shadow of a line of willows. He took a last look at the men clustered near the fire, then softly walked towards the picket line.

Shedd moved cautiously and only after Vernell rejoined the others did he venture to mount and ride out of the tiny oval.

Buck Shedd cared naught for what Vernell might do. The young outlaw was just brag and no guts to back it up with.

But he was a careful man. His years of riding the owlhoot trail had made him that way. No sense taking chances now, even with the kid.

Shedd emerged from the canyon and now a buoying confidence eroded his caution. A quick glance around the dark hills showed nothing. Shedd spurred his mount into a swift gallop.

What he failed to notice was Adam Brewer, dry camped just off the trail.

Adam listened to the fading hoofbeats. He wondered about the night rider as he laid aside his rifle. One of the rustlers heading back towards town, he surmised correctly and snuggled back under his blanket.

Now what was up? Oh, well, first things first, he mused. Catch up to the herd in the morning. But then what?

He would just have to match his great strength against their numbers. Maybe this one would run into the law and a posse. Sure hope they get here in time to help. And with this comforting thought, Adam went back to sleep.

Shedd felt a flagging tiredness. It made him cross and irritated with his lagging steed. He dipped out of Turkey Creek several miles below the Circle B figuring that this ruse would throw off any would-be trackers.

He spurred his horse cruelly. By this time night had turned to morning. A hard-driving mile slid away under his worn-out bay before Shedd relented. He reined up just below the crest of a gently rising hill and let the foam-flecked beast blow.

Shedd strode impatiently to the hilltop. From its vantage point, he could just make out the blurred outlines of Raton. A stir of dust off to his right caught Shedd's attention.

He faded behind a short stand of cedars. Even in the distance, there was no mistaking the high, beanpole figure of Jack Lester. And flanking him was some dried-out Circle B rider.

Shedd squinted against the glaring sun. But the other half-dozen or so men were just indistinct objects as they bobbed along.

Raton drowsed under the hot sun. A wide banner that proclaimed the big rodeo drooped listlessly in anticipation of a huge celebration later today.

The streets appeared deserted. But Shedd avoided riding directly into town. Once more his hard-earned caution overrode a reckless urge to pin Ross down on their deal. How he would manage that, Shedd did not know just yet.

Maybe the threat of exposing his cover, Shedd thought. Wouldn't that bunch of ninnies in town be surprised to learn that Stanley Ross was not such an upstanding citizen, after all?

The bay stumbled and almost went down. Shedd jerked him to a halt. He stepped out of the saddle.

A small gully beckoned. Here Shedd dumped his saddle and turned the wind-broken horse loose.

Shedd followed the brushy little draw until

it bisected the back lot of Joe Henson's livery stable. He paused for just a moment and, not seeing any signs of movement, scrambled up a sandy bank.

A lone horse stood head down in the corral. It switched at flies and showed no apparent interest in the man who walked with long-reaching strides into a shaded alley.

Buck Shedd didn't hesitate once he gained this meager cover. He tugged his hat low and emerged from the alley to walk with purposeful steps towards Ross's store.

Shedd entered the dim building. He passed the old clerk, Hawkins. "Ross in today?"

"He's in his office, Mr. Shedd," Hawkins said.

"Good." Shedd jerked a thumb, pointing to the front door. "Go get a beer. Lock the door on your way out," he ordered. "If anyone asks, you ain't seen me. Take the day off."

"Yes, sir, Mr. Shedd." Hawkins trembled with fear. He scuttled around the counter to do the outlaw's bidding.

Ross looked up from a column of figures when the door opened. He frowned at his unwelcome visitor.

"You don't seem overly glad to see me, partner." Buck Shedd grinned.

"I'm not," Ross flatly stated. "Why aren't

you on the way to Durango with the herd?"

"Reckon you and me have some unfinished business." Shedd's voice was harsh.

"Such as what?" Ross asked, more than slightly puzzled.

"The Rafter W. I want it now," Shedd asked.

"But the bank note is not due yet. I can't foreclose until it is. You know that. And until I do, you'll just have to wait." Ross leaned back in his chair with a self-satisfied air.

"No dice, Ross. I'm tired of sneakin' up an alley and stayin' out of sight. From now on, I'm ridin' straight into town. And as a big ranch owner, ain't nobody goin' to say or do anything to me. You call in all those debts you been braggin' about and I'll do the rest."

Ross jerked forward. His eyes shifted inadvertently to a half-opened desk drawer. A shaft of sunlight glinted off the little derringer.

He hastily looked away, but the slight change in his expression was not lost to Buck Shedd. He read the merchant's eyes, noting a new confidence. His body coiled in readiness.

"Hmmm." Ross appeared to think over his henchman's orders. I'll get him now, when he's off guard, Ross thought.

He shuffled some papers, pretending to store

them in the desk. His hand closed over the derringer. It felt cold, hard, and ready to kill.

Ross swept the small gun up, swinging it towards Shedd. Suddenly, he froze. A small gasp started to form on his gaping mouth.

Shedd hadn't seemed to move, but a big black-muzzled Colt stared into his face.

Ross's pig eyes opened wide, staring like glossy round marbles, as a sheet of flame spewed from Shedd's gun.

Ross slammed back in his chair. His huge belly grumbled for a moment. Then he sat still, staring blankly at nothing.

The muffled report died away. A thin trail of powder smoke drifted lazily upwards from the Colt's muzzle. It left behind a lingering acrid odor.

Buck Shedd holstered the big revolver. A malicious smile hovered around the corners of his mouth.

He riffled the desk with practiced hands. The invoices that Ross had been working on were tossed aside. His questing gaze rested on several sheets of paper that lay in the second drawer down.

Grain, flour, canned goods, and several lesser items were listed. But it was April Winters's signature that caught and held his attention.

He swept up the papers, along with a column of figures that was under them. His breath caught at the staggering amount that was owed Ross by the Rafter W. A satisfied smile built, then slowly died away as a new thought hit Shedd.

How to use them now that Ross was dead? He lifted a cigar from Ross's pocket and sat down on the edge of the desk. Several minutes passed. Shedd puffed pensively on the expensive cigar.

Many ideas raced through his head only to be culled as unworkable. But one vague thought kept returning to his mind.

Seemed like sometime back he remembered Al Hayes talking quietly by their campfire one night. It was the only time that he could ever remember the grotesque little outlaw mentioning his past.

Yes, that was it, Shedd remembered. His usually calm pulse jumped with a budding excitement. Hayes, as he recalled, had been sent to the pen for forgery!

Shedd enlarged his idea. He would wait for dark, then slip out of town. When Hayes returned, he would have the man draw up a will.

And since Shedd had been seen a few times with Ross, he would explain that they were half brothers and that there were no other living relatives.

That would explain his relationship with Ross. With that accomplished, he could then move to take over the Rafter W.

But he still needed a copy of Ross's signature. Shedd slid off the desk. He started to resume the search when his eyes fell upon an invoice that lay by his feet. There, big as life, was the signature he needed.

"Good thing you have to sign for this stuff when you receive it," he grunted to the dead man. "Makes it that much easier for me. Heck, these clods around here will never know the difference. And Stanley Ross not bein' your real name, ain't nobody goin' to come forward and argue with me."

Chapter Thirteen

An accidental fall from his horse had left
Dan Martin unconscious for several hours.
But, luckily, he was not harmed. Dan Martin
now paced his gelding easily. Once he crossed
a shallow, sandy wash. Here, even to his less-
than-expert eye, were the deep impressions
left by two fast-moving horses.

He lifted the gelding into a swinging canter
after crossing the wash. Horse and rider cast
one long shadow over the ground.

Dan pulled his hat down. He peered out from
under the lowered brim.

The trail he rode was dim, in reality no more
than a trace. But the tracks remained. He followed them up a low-rising hill and pulled to
a stop.

A quick survey proved the darkening willows along Turkey Creek to be deserted. The fresh tracks under his own mount showed where April had paused earlier.

Dan grinned with a great satisfaction. He clucked the sorrel into motion following April's tracks down the hill.

Just inside the willows boundary, Dan found a scuffed area. He studied the marks, barely able to make them out in the quickly gathering dusk. Then his search was rewarded. One light moccasin print approached the disturbed ground. He found another print further along. This one was deeper, embedded in the soft dirt as if its maker carried a heavy burden.

Two sets of horse tracks lined out, heading due west from the creek. One he was sure belonged to April's rangy bay.

Dan whistled happily. He dismounted from the sorrel and picketed him in a thick clump of grass. Full dark settled in while he gathered driftwood for a fire.

Soon a tiny flame flickered against the night. Dan put a can of water on to boil. He shaved several strips from a slab of bacon and placed them in a skillet.

The water boiled up. Dan tossed a meager handful of coffee grounds into the can. He watched the water bubble and roil as it turned brown. The bacon sizzled.

Dan pushed the coffee to one side, letting the grounds settle while he dug a hard biscuit out of his grub sack. He eyed the bacon. It was done to a neat turn and gave off a savory odor.

Out in the darkness the gelding circled towards the campfire. He munched contentedly on the lush grass. The sounds of his chewing were a comfort to the lonely camper. No other sounds broke the stillness of this night.

Dan drank his coffee straight from the can. He used his fingers to pick the bacon out of the skillet. Then he sopped up the bacon grease with the biscuit.

After this simple repast, Dan rinsed out the utensils in the creek. He drank deep from the clear, swift-running water.

He strolled slowly back to the now low-burning fire. The sky began to brighten as a near full moon started its ascent.

Dan rolled a quirley. He lounged back on his bedroll watching the stars wink overhead. The fire burned down until only a few small red embers remained.

The gelding stood quiet now, head down, as he rested. Along the creek bank several frogs croaked in unison.

His dark thoughts turned to the job ahead. Maybe tomorrow there would be the break that he was waiting for.

Despite his serious thoughts, Dan's eyelids grew heavy with sleep. He tossed away the long-since-burned-out stub of his quirley and slid into a deep, restless slumber.

The next day dawned clear and cool. But even before Dan had brewed fresh coffee and used it to rinse down another hard biscuit, there was a promise of the heat to come.

He saddled the restive sorrel and lashed on the bedroll well before full sunrise. Already a thin scum of sweat beaded his whisker-darkened cheeks.

Dan gathered up the reins. He stood with one hand gripping the saddle horn.

But he did not immediately swing into the hull. Instead, he waited a moment, debating which direction to take.

Dan shrugged and moved into the saddle. Again, he paused before lifting the reins.

A thought entered his mind. He decided to head west, again trailing after Pike Moore and his unwilling companion. And of course he would keep his eyes open for other people.

Two hours later the sun was a blazing ball that bore down upon the rider's back. His shirt became sticky with sweat. Now the ground started to rise and pitch sharply upwards. The sorrel grunted mightily as he jumped up one particularly steep ridge. He slid precariously down the back slope, forelegs stiff, and rump almost skimming the ground.

Dan reined his trembling mount to a stop at the bottom. He found that he was also trembling after the sudden and swift sliding descent.

A shaky hand reached for the makings in his shirt pocket. Maybe a cigarette would help to calm his nerves, Dan hoped.

And help it did. Dan idly inspected the surrounding area as he smoked. He appeared to be in a wide, rough-bottomed gully that ran north to south.

From where he sat, the other side seemed inaccessible.

He slumped over the saddle horn. Dan had about made up his mind to turn south, taking the easy way out, when his idly roving gaze turned to the gully's rock-strewn bottom.

The fresh, two-horse trail he was following petered out. His brow furrowed with a puzzled frown. He could make out that several head of cattle had recently been driven up the gully. Their tracks and those of several riders completely blotted out Pike Moore's trail.

Dan stepped out of the saddle. He ground reined the sorrel and walked gingerly around a slick boulder.

He knelt to study this new development at closer range. From the tracks he could tell that the stock was being pushed hard, even over this treacherous ground.

His hand spanned a fresh hoofprint. Only now was the sand running down its sides. Dan couldn't be sure, but it looked like four, maybe five, riders pushing the herd.

But to where? There was nothing but the mountains ahead. Probably, he decided, this gully branched off into a side canyon. But where could it lead?

This had to be rustlers, Dan guessed. They had finally made their move.

If only he could get help. But almost everyone would be in Raton, and Raton was too far away.

He would have to trail them by himself. That would be mighty risky business, Dan thought. But right at this moment there didn't seem to be any other way for him to go.

Yes, he would have to trail the rustlers alone and somehow figure out a way to recover the stolen stock. How he could accomplish this, Dan had no idea at the moment.

Anyway, it stacked up that he was only one man against four, maybe more men. He had been in tight spots before, but not against such strong odds.

Still, somehow he would just have to finish the job himself. Or, more probably, the job would finish him.

Chapter Fourteen

Dan Martin followed the trail as long as he could. But then in the dark he lost the trail completely. He turned around, heading for home, but soon he was surprised to find himself outside Pike Moore's cabin.

A mule brayed raucously. Dan stopped the near-spent gelding. He could feel the mule's presence, following him like a curious watchdog.

"Hello the house," he called out, not wishing to be mistaken for a raider. He slid wearily out of the saddle.

From nowhere, a strong hand gripped his arm. "Easy, boy," a rough voice said into his ear.

Dan stumbled over the threshold. He heard the door shut softly behind him.

The tiniest flicker of coals came from a fireplace. Slowly his eyes adjusted to the dim cabin light.

The barrel of a rifle glinted. It pointed directly at him.

For a single heartstopping moment, he expected it to belch flame. His stomach knotted. The tantalizing odor of coffee filled his nostrils making his mouth water.

But would he live to taste it? Who was here and where did that wolfer vanish?

"Ease off the trigger, April. It's my friend, Dan Martin," came Pike Moore's harsh voice from right behind his elbow.

He heard the slight click as a rifle hammer was adjusted.

"Huh. Some friend you pick." April's voice sounded like music to Dan's ears. Never would he have, in his wildest thoughts, imagined that he would be glad to see her.

Pike Moore cast a speculative eye on the worn-out figure of Dan Martin. "Have a sit down," Pike said, motioning to the table. "Strike up a light, April."

Pike lifted a huge fire-blackened coffeepot

from the glowing coals. "What brings you ramming around these mountains this time of night?" Pike queried.

"Rustlers," Dan answered. He cradled a steaming cup of the thick black brew in both hands.

"Huh!" April snorted. "We've always had them. They're just a piddlin' nuisance."

"I'm afraid not this time," Dan replied. "From the size of the swath that they cut, I'd say they just about cleaned out your north range." He described the route he had followed until he had lost the trail.

"Did that last canyon have a right pert-sized creek running out of it?" Pike asked.

"It sure did. And the mouth was all brush-choked. Do you know where it is?" Dan asked.

"Yep. That particular canyon leads out towards the big pass. Durango ain't too much farther on north. Got a railroad there, so the rustlers don't have too much trouble unloading their drives, big or small."

Pike paused to consider. "About when do you figure they hit the canyon?"

"Not long before dark." Dan answered. He thought for a moment. "Had to be, 'cause I could still smell dust in the air."

April Winters sat down heavily. She looked across the table, appraising him with an openly frank stare. When she finally spoke, the words came low and were almost lost to the tired man's ears.

"What were you doing out on the range? I thought you had orders to stay at the ranch."

Dan nodded. "I did. But that was impossible after all that's been happening lately." He smiled. "Everything all right between you two?"

Pike Moore guffawed. "Sure is. April's not so bad when you show her who's boss. She give you a rough time?"

"Fair to middling," Dan said. "Right now I feel like a failure. There was a while I had a crazy notion that me and Miss Spring might get married someday. But, heck, she deserves better than me."

"Oh, you're not so bad." April smiled. "Just can't even get out of bed right is all."

This sally hurt Dan's pride. "There is something that I've been doing a good job at. Until today, anyhow."

"Oh, yes? And what is that?" April asked.

"I reckon it's all right to tell you now. I'm a range detective. Captain Franklin got drift of too much rustling in these parts. And the governor wanted to stop it. Only this time Franklin didn't have one of his experienced men available, so I got stuck with the job."

Dan paused for breath. April was stunned by the revelation that this inept cowhand could be any kind of a range detective.

Pike Moore merely nodded. He drummed his fingers on the table, lost in deep thought.

"You ain't actually a real lawman," Pike stated.

"No," Dan admitted. "I've helped clear up some small problems before, but none like this. I honestly don't know what I would have done if I'd have caught up with those rustlers."

"I've been thinkin' about them," Pike said. "It should take just about all night to drive through that canyon. I doubt if they will push that hard, though. Then it's a good half a day's hard goin' to reach the big pass.

"If we leave here at first light and cut straight for the pass, we can maybe beat them there. Best get a little sleep so as to be fresh in the morning."

"But there's only two of us and four or five in that bunch," Dan said.

"Three of us," April stated positively. "And

I'm better than any pair of no-good two-bit rustlers."

Dan glanced at Pike Moore. But that worthy only grinned and nodded his head in approval.

A hard hand shook Dan awake. He rolled out of his blanket with a groan.

The pines sighed overhead. A lightening in the sky showed that dawn would not be long in coming.

"Rustle, cowboy," Pike Moore ordered brusquely. "Coffee's on. By the time you wrap yourself around a cup and some hardtack, I'll have your saddle on old Don."

"Don?" Dan looked around the tiny meadow, but all he could see were two long-eared mules. "A mule? Me ride one of them contrary devils?"

"You bet," Pike answered, sounding very serious. "Ain't nothin' better nor more sure-footed for mountain-climbing except a goat."

"Huh?" Dan snorted in disbelief. "Reckon I'd rather be a-horseback."

"Not today. Your sorrel's come up lame. He's limpin' pretty bad on his left foreleg. Probably stepped in a hole last night and pulled a tendon.

"Anyway, you and ole Don ought to get along just fine. He's quite a bit older than Pete and not nearly so fractious."

"Yeow. Lord help me." Dan headed for the cabin, muttering to himself. Dang if he didn't have the darnedest luck.

He cast a jaundiced eye at the mules. One gray-muzzled beast flicked an ear at him, as if to say, Just wait until you get closer.

The mule's lips peeled back and a mocking hee-haw followed Dan into the cabin.

Which one was that? he worried. Not Don, he hoped.

Chapter Fifteen

The big rodeo was over and now Chuck Raines felt drained of all emotion after its high-spirited excitement. As darkness crept in over Raton, he made his slow way to a big house near the outskirts of town.

There lived the Benson couple, old friends of the Winters family. Theirs was the most imposing house around. Benson owned the local bank—or, from what Chuck Raines could gather, now only ran it for that Stanley Ross dude.

He hitched up the sling on his broken left arm. That old cayuse, Thunder, he had drawn to ride should have been named Dynamite, Chuck thought ruefully. He approached the front door and rapped smartly.

"Howdy, Mrs. Benson." He swept off his huge stetson and made a clumsy bow. "And how are you this fine evening?"

A smiling laugh from the old woman rewarded his efforts. "Come on in, Chuck. I suppose you're here to see Summer."

"Yes. But only because such a lovely creature as you are already hitched," Chuck teased.

"Get on with you, cowboy. Can't you ever be serious?"

"Maybe. It all depends." A twinkle lighted his wide gray eyes, but he did not elaborate on what would make him serious.

Mrs. Benson led the way through a small sitting room to a huge parlor. Although Chuck knew the old couple fairly well, this was the first time he had been inside the big, rambling house.

June Winters sat languidly in front of an empty fireplace. Doggone, Chuck thought, she sure is pretty. No wonder Jack was hell bent on marrying her.

Spring paced restlessly before a side window. She spoke to the tall cowboy, but soon withdrew into her own thoughts.

Mrs. Benson indicated a plump couch. "Sit down, Chuck," she said.

Summer strode into the room just then, dressed in a short jacket and men's denims. An impish grin lighted her face at the sight of Raines.

"Well, hello there," she giggled. "Did you eat anymore dust today, Chuck?"

"Naw. Say you should try it sometime. Ain't bad." He could not suppress a boyish humor upon seeing her.

"Huh. Not me," Summer said. "I would have stayed aboard that plug. Why, he couldn't buck no more than an old plow horse." Her teasing words only served to stir his interest in this long-legged tomboy.

"I bet you could, at that," Chuck said. He felt expansive on this night and nothing she said could insult him or injure his manly pride.

An afterthought struck him. "Where is everyone?" His gaze traveled around the room questioningly.

"Didn't you hear while you were out salving your dignity with a bottle of whiskey?" Summer retorted. "Jasper from the Circle B came in. There was a big raid on the spread. Jack and several of the boys headed out earlier to help Jasper track down the rustlers. Mr. Benson went with the posse."

"Why, that old warrior," Chuck said. "He shouldn't be out there rammin' around in those hills."

"My feelings exactly," Mrs. Benson retorted. "A man of his age traipsing off to chase outlaws." But despite her sharp words, a thread of worry crept through her voice.

Summer continued. "One of Adam's hands was shot. May stayed at the ranch to take care of him. Autumn couldn't stand being left out of all the excitement and took off to be with May."

"April?" Chuck turned a questioning glance on Spring.

"We haven't heard," Summer hastily answered. "Come on. Let's go for a walk. Or is it too much beneath a cowboy's pride to stroll in the garden?"

"After you." Chuck swept wide his hat. Once outside, he added, "I'd walk through Hades to be with you. Summer Winters, doggone it, when are you goin' to relent and be Summer Raines?"

"Be serious," the young girl replied. "Couldn't you see that Spring was upset?"

"Huh? I am serious. What's botherin' Spring?" Chuck asked.

"Her cowboy, Dan, is alone at the ranch. She's afraid that the rustlers might have hit there also. It's the not knowing for sure that's bothering her," Summer answered. She placed a hand on his good arm.

Her strong grip surprised him. "Maybe when this is all over," she added softly.

Chuck's heart sang. He felt capable of any deed. "You run and tell Miss Spring not to worry. I'll slope on down to Henson's livery, get my horse, then head out to the ranch and see how old Dan is makin' out."

"Oh, would you? I know it will sure make Spring feel better if she knows that Dan is all right," Summer burst out happily. Then her quick smile suddenly faded. "But your arm? Won't it bother you?"

"Naw. Been hurt worse than this and still worked cattle," Chuck reassured the girl.

"All right, but you wait. I'll go help you saddle up." And before he could say another word, she swiftly disappeared somewhere.

Chuck Raines tugged a sack of makings from his shirt pocket. He opened the tobacco pouch with his teeth. As he started to fumble with the thin sheets of paper, Summer reappeared just as swiftly as she had vanished.

"Here, cowboy. Let me do that for you."And she deftly spun a neat cylinder together. "Spring sure perked up. You don't know how much she appreciates what you're doing."

"Say."

A puzzled frown furrowed the cowboy's brow. "How come you can spin smoke like that?"

"Nothing to it. Just another one of my many cowboy accomplishments." Summer tossed her pretty head.

Buck Shedd rummaged through Ross's living quarters. Upon not finding anything that told who Ross actually was, or where he had come from before arriving in Raton, Shedd let himself out the back door.

The alleyway was already as dark as the inside of a tomb. A few stars twinkled overhead. Shedd paused to let his eyes adjust. He considered his next move and only then did an annoying tiredness drag at his shoulders.

Shedd blinked red-rimmed eyes and shook off the tired feeling. There was yet much to be done. He must be out of town and down at his small place when they found Ross's body.

An evil grimace covered his whisker-stubbled face. It would be just another unsolved murder. He would come forward and take over.

Maybe his half brother, poor old Stanley, had been robbed.

Shedd chuckled low in his chest, but there was no mirth in the sound. He must have a horse and, since Joe Henson's livery seemed the most logical place, Shedd padded out of the alley. He cut a direct path to the stable.

Once there, though, he paused again in the heavy structure's deep shadows. A lantern burned just inside the front entrance. Not far up the street, Shedd made out the shape of two punchers strolling leisurely towards the livery.

He squinted, trying to place them. One carried an arm in a sling and from his high carriage, Shedd hazarded a guess that this was Raines, the Rafter W foreman.

The other, shorter, slender form caught and held his attention. He puzzled over its identity for a moment.

Suddenly, a tinkling laugh drifted on the quiet night air. Shedd felt his hands shake violently for a quick second. He calmed his frayed nerves and grew icy calm.

It came to him then. From the height and slim-waisted figure, this had to be Summer Winters!

Shedd ground his teeth together. Why not

have it all? he thought. There were places back in the wilderness that even he did not know about.

The outlaw felt no qualms about kidnapping the girl. Many times he had seen her riding the range and he had been sorely tempted.

A hue and cry would go out. Posses would scour the countryside. For a woman was next to sacred in this country made up almost entirely of hard-riding punchers.

He would ride with the posses, deep into the woods. But always to no avail. No one would ever know.

Shedd flattened himself against the stable wall. He waited, patient once more, until their soft footfalls entered the low-roofed structure.

A supreme confidence carried him to the wide front door. One quick look both ways from his slitted eyes found the street still empty.

Tonight was perfect, he thought. Most of the riders were out with the posse chasing rustlers. Everybody else was tired from the big Fourth of July celebration.

Shedd slipped the thong off his Colt and lifted the weapon smoothly from its well-oiled holster. He stepped into the stable.

Summer lifted a knee into the mustang's

barrel. He grunted and expelled his breath.
She jerked the cinch tight with practiced
hands.

"Hold it, Raines," Shedd murmured as the
startled cowboy spotted him. "Good job, girlie.
Now lead out that black and throw a saddle
on him." He edged away from the lantern,
placing himself in the shadows.

Summer balked. "I will not," she retorted.

"Sure you will, or I'll finish off your cowboy
here." Shedd wagged the Colt suggestively.

Summer glanced at Chuck.

"Do as he says," the cowboy advised. "Say,
ain't you Buck Shedd? Just what's your game?"

"Me and Miss Winters here are goin' for a
little ride." Shedd could not resist bragging a
little. "Reckon time we get back she'll appreciate what a fine upstanding citizen I am."

"No way! I'm not going anywhere with you!"
Summer burst out. Suddenly, she slipped out
of sight behind the black.

Chuck Raines knew he had to try for his
gun. Shedd would never ride out and leave
him alive to tell about this.

His hand clawed for the big-butted revolver
on his hip. At the same time he leaped to his
left to sprawl full length on the stable floor.
His gun came up. Too late!

The muzzle of Shedd's Colt had tracked him and now it centered on his prone form. He could see Shedd laughing.

Chuck Raines rolled over, desperately trying to clear his Colt. Pain flooded his shattered arm and left him weak and nauseous. He blinked into the Colt's ominous bore as Shedd squeezed the trigger.

A spiteful crack sounded and a small flash came from under the black horse's belly. The animal gave a frightened squeal and jerked loose to go running headlong out of the stable.

Shedd staggered slightly. He clamped a hand to his side and felt moisture. Dang woman shot me! he thought in amazement. He swung his Colt towards Summer. By the devil, if he couldn't take her, a bullet would!

The small-caliber pistol cracked again and Shedd flinched as a whining bullet tugged at his ear. His Colt spat lead, but his aim was thrown way off. Somewhere a stall splintered under the heavy slug.

Raines had his gun up. The madly racing black cleared the door, exposing Shedd's high frame. Raines got off a shot just as Shedd fired at Summer.

He fired again, liking the feel as his Colt bucked and rocked in his grip. A muffled curse came from the hard-hit outlaw. Shedd's Colt steadied, aiming at Summer.

The heavy report of Raines's pistol overrode the spiteful crack of Summer's small handgun. Shedd's gun dipped. Very slowly he buckled at the knees.

The grim-visaged outlaw fell loosely. A tiny puff of dust rose around his limp body.

A stunning quiet settled in as a racketing horse ceased to kick at his stall.

"You all right, Summer?" Fear for the girl's safety squeezed at Chuck's chest.

"I—I think so," Summer choked. Her pale face made a white oval as she leaned back, weak and spent, on a stack of hay.

Raines cautiously approached the outlaw's still form. His warm Colt trailed in one big fist. He rolled Shedd over and gave one swift glance at the dead man.

Something white half spilled from Shedd's vest pocket. Raines knelt and lifted out a half-dozen sheets of paper.

He read the notes signed by April. But a regular invoice to Ross's store, from a hardware company in Ohio, puzzled him.

"Now what do you make of this?" he mused aloud. "What is this ranny doin' with Ross's notes on the Rafter W?"

Summer peered over his shoulder. Her eyes were big orbs in a still very pale face.

"Gee," she whispered. "I didn't know that we owed old man Ross so much money. Why, I bet there's enough there to take us over."

"Say, you might have something there," Raines agreed. "Without a herd to sell off this fall, the ranch would be stone broke." He jerked erect, holstering his Colt.

"Summer, you get someone to check on Ross. Now I've got to find out what's been happening on the range."

He turned towards the saddled horse and noticed a small group of townspeople carefully approaching the stable. A wave of his hand brought them on in.

"There's Hawkins." Raines had spied the store clerk. "Send him to check."

The nervous mustang was eager to leave this place. Raines led him out to the street and swung into the saddle.

The mustang's coiled muscles exploded. He burst into a headlong run before Raines had completely settled into the saddle.

Chapter Sixteen

Dan Martin didn't quite know how to take the little mountain mule. It seemed docile enough when he climbed aboard.

"Get up, Don." Dan kicked the mule lightly with his heels. He didn't know for sure what reaction he expected. But the beast only waggled his long ears and fell into line behind April's rawboned bay.

Up ahead Pike Moore led the way. His long legs dangled ludicrously below his mule's low body.

Pike set a steady, if not fast, pace cutting over the hills. He knew these ranges better than most people did their own front yards.

The miles fell behind as they climbed higher. Once they crossed a narrow hogbacked ridge and turned to follow its course.

Don trotted along smartly. His short legs came down hard, jolting Dan until he just knew that every bone in his body was broken.

Never again, Dan vowed in passionate silence, would he climb on top of a mule, much less this particular one.

The ridge climbed upwards. The pace slowed. Dan glanced ahead and saw that Pike was some distance ahead. April's big range horse was having difficulty keeping its footing. It lagged, forcing them to fall farther behind.

The bay stumbled and almost threw April over its head. She jerked him back into line with a curse that any cowboy could well appreciate.

Dan gritted his teeth as he hit a tricky twist along the ridge. His legs clamped tight around the mule.

But Don merely squatted lower and leaped upwards. His nimble hooves dug into the ground and he negotiated the trail with hardly any extra effort.

Dan began to understand now why Pike liked the little animals for this rough travel. "Maybe," he grudgingly admitted, urging Don onward, "you ain't too awful bad after all."

The ridge curved slightly, pinching out as

it ran together with a higher timber-studded mountain range.

Pike disappeared into a stand of stunted cedars where the two ridges formed a vee. April's bay continued to struggle as he strained upwards.

Don suddenly took the bit into his teeth. He seemed impatient at trailing the horse and, with tiny hooves digging hard, he trotted effortlessly into the cedars.

Pike's mule waited, tied securely to a gnarled tree. Don trotted up to him and nipped at his flank. He turned a wall-eyed look on Don and one hoof flicked out.

Dan hastily departed from Don's back. Pike came gliding back through the cedars. A satisfied look made him smile. He tore off a big bite of tobacco, and at Dan's negative shake of the head, the plug disappeared into his shirt front.

April came into the cedars, dragging her horse. She stopped some distance from the mules and ground hitched the cow pony.

The leggy April puffed mightily from this unaccustomed exertion. Her bay stood head down and flanks quivering. Don looked quizzically at the spent horse as if to say, Why are you tired? I'm just now heated up and ready to go.

April glared at Dan. "Smart aleck," she said testily.

Dan spread wide his arms. "Wasn't me. That mule took it upon himself. He got tired of trailin' that clumsy cayuse of yours, I guess."

Pike leaned on his rifle. "Boy, you two sure rub each other the wrong way." He spat, then continued. "Ain't no time for bickerin' now. The big pass is just over this little notch."

Dan hitched up his gun belt. "Did we beat the rustlers here?" he asked.

Pike shrugged. "Can't say for sure, but if they're pushin' real hard, they should be along soon. Too much grass and timber to make out any dust from the herd. Dan, you ain't brought no rifle." He paused to consider this. "Range dick, huh? Any good with that hogleg?"

"Some," Dan answered, grinning.

"April, get your rifle," Pike ordered. "The pass ain't too wide once you get into it. Might be best if you get up high and cover us from the rocks. When we hit the bottom, I'll hole up where it starts to narrow. Dan, you fort up forty, fifty yards above me. I'll open the ball soon as the drag comes even with my position.

Now we better rattle our hocks so's to be ready."

Bridle bits were quickly slipped out of the animals' mouths. Feedbags were put over their noses to keep them eating and quiet.

The pass resembled a wide-toed, high-buttoned shoe, Dan thought. The entrance sloped gently upward. It arched slightly and then some upheaval of nature had caused it to climb very sharply upwards.

The rough sides pinched in. They were dotted with huge boulders. Here and there a straggling cedar clung tenaciously to the walls.

April struggled laboriously to a vantage point high in the pass.

At this spot the pass did not flatten before it slanted down the other side. A knifelike spine humped up sharply. Here the herd would have to funnel down to walk two abreast. The cattle, footsore and worn out, would have to be forced up and over this barrier that a fickle nature had placed within the pass.

A rock bounded down the slope. It hit bottom with a dull thud. April disappeared from sight. A serene stillness settled over the pass.

Dan snuggled in behind a jagged boulder. He peered around its comforting edge, but nothing stirred. Pike Moore had long since vanished, forting up somewhere down below.

The sun passed its zenith. Its warming rays fell upon Dan's back and made him drowsy.

"Hey, this won't do." He jerked wide awake.

Dan rolled over and cast a judicious eye at the clear sky. It sure was a nice day, he mused. Racing thoughts made him go cold inside. A clammy film of moisture shone along his whisker-darkened jaws.

This just might be his last day alive, Dan suddenly realized. He wondered what the next few hours would bring.

The Colt gouged him in the hip. A rock lizard hurried along. It stopped short to stare at the human that dared invade his domain. His neck pumped like a bellows. Dan flipped a pebble and the lizard scuttled away.

Now that reptile was wondering what I'm doing here, he mused silently. Truth is, so am I. Why, if it wasn't for Spring, I'd have looked up old Marshal McCoy, then lit out of Raton at a high lope. Heck, I ain't no hero. Don't suppose life would be much worth living, though, without Spring.

For a moment Dan wished mightily that he had not met such a fine young woman. And the wonder of it all was that she cared for him, too! This thought kept him rooted to the rocks.

The aggravated bawling of a tired calf came faintly to his hearing. He peered around the boulder's rough edge.

An honest measure of fear squeezed at his insides. The Colt nestled in the palm of his hand and he did not realize when he had fisted the pistol.

Two riders suddenly popped out of a timbered draw. A stream of cattle followed almost immediately upon their horses' heels.

Dan picked out two more riders, one on each side flanking the herd. There would be one, maybe two, bringing up the rear to push the stragglers along, he theorized.

One big-hatted rustler turned aside. He sat watching the herd file by as he built a quirley.

The other rider, a gnomelike figure, astride a big brute of a blue roan, forged ahead. He spurred into a gallop to enter the pass well in advance of the tired cattle.

Dan waited as the vile-looking outlaw rode past, just below his position. The blue roan snorted and Al Hayes shuttled a baleful stare straight into Dan Martin's eyes. Dan tore his eyes away, knowing for sure that he had been seen.

Where in the devil was Pike Moore? he worried. The last cow straggled into view. A slim young rider slashed viciously at its rump, forcing it into a lumbering run.

The incline turned steeply upwards. Already the lead cow was slowing as she tried to balk. The members of the herd shoved at their leader. The big-hatted rustler wheeled about.

Al Hayes did not feel right when he entered the pass. He had ridden too many dark and dangerous trails not to know when something was amiss.

He forged ahead. When the big roan snorted and shied slightly to his right, Hayes automatically glanced in the other direction. A flash of movement behind a huge boulder caught his attention.

Hayes started to spin the roan. His mouth opened to shout a warning as his six-gun cleared leather, swinging towards the huge boulder!

Pike Moore suddenly stepped out of the brush. He had taken up a position that placed him opposite Dan, but somewhat lower down. Just to his front and a little left, a large-boled pine offered him cover if the rustlers refused to surrender.

As the drag rider appeared, he called to the flanker who now rode within a few feet from him, "Hands up! You're covered front and center." The command rang loud and clear, carrying above the muted shuffle of the herd.

Bud Stone froze when the harsh voice rang out almost at his side. His hands shot skyward.

Tim Alvin pivoted his cow pony. His pistol swept up, seeking a target. One sweeping glance took in the still figure of Bud Stone. He placed the buckskin figure of Pike Moore directly across the herd. His finger tightened on the trigger.

But Pike Moore glided swiftly to cover. His rifle came up to center on the rustler's vest. He fired once and saw that the heavy slug's impact ripped Alvin from the saddle.

Bark jumped from the pine. A pistol coughed. Another bullet went spinning off through the tree limbs.

Pike slid around the huge tree. Dang fool, he thought, and held his fire as Tom Vernell charged through the trees. The young rustler fired again, shooting wildly from the back of his racing pony.

The muzzle of Pike's rifle came up. Vernell cleared a thin stand of pine and now rode in the open. Pike sighed and fired at the rapidly approaching rider. A satisfying jolt hit his shoulder. Smoke billowed from the muzzle of his rifle.

Tom Vernell was hit bad. He stood straight up in the stirrups. His maddened pony suddenly swerved and the young rustler pitched headlong to the ground. He bounced twice and rolled several feet until his momentum was finally arrested.

Bud Stone saw his chance. As the mountain man turned to meet Vernell's challenge, he tucked tail and ran.

Stone slammed home the spurs. He turned back, riding bent over the saddle horn as he strove to reach the relative safety that a nearby draw offered.

April Winters held a steady bead on the little rider as he entered the pass. Slowly she took up the slack on the trigger.

Suddenly, he veered and a pistol appeared in his fist. April pulled the trigger.

Her shot blended with Pike's. Shattering echoes bounced up and down the pass. She levered another round into the chamber of her carbine.

But Al Hayes sudden shift had thrown off April's aim. Her bullet smacked into the blue roan's head. He went down hard. Hayes leaped nimbly aside and scuttled into the rocks.

A whining slug gave impetus to his retreat. Dan squinted through thick powder smoke and knew that he had missed. He fired again just for good measure as the little outlaw vanished, and saw rocks chip and fly at the man's heels.

Something tugged at Dan's sleeve. A stinging pain sliced at his arm. Dust jumped from the crown of his hat as it flew up from his head.

Dan flopped back behind the boulder and knew that he was in serious trouble. The big-hatted outlaw! Where was he?

He wiggled around to take a look and directly across from him as the little outlaw cut loose.

April fired again and drove Hayes back to cover. He nested up in a jumble of rocks. Hayes scanned the wall above and ahead of his position.

Trapped! he realized. For an almost sheer upthrust of slick rock met his searching gaze.

From somewhere below he heard Carl Tucker let loose a round. He debated a zigzagging retreat back down out of the pass.

But another rifle boomed from far below.

Hayes studied the report and knew from its duller roar that this was not Tucker's Winchester.

Whipsawed! he now realized. But by whom? And who was that ranny just across the pass from him? Now if he could just dart over to that side.

Hayes mulled over this idea. Just might work, he thought. That galoot didn't seem to be too good a shot. Once across, he could take that one out of action.

And then the rifleman up above couldn't see him. Maybe he could slide back down behind that wide-spreading cedar over there.

His course of action now decided upon, Hayes waited out the tense minutes. When Tucker fires again, I'll go, he thought.

The minutes ticked away, finally building into a long drawn-out hour. Still, Hayes waited. Where was Tucker now? he wondered.

As long shadows fell over the pass, Hayes figured his chances to be even better. Tucker must be dead or captured, he finally decided. Suddenly, an entirely new thought dawned upon him.

Where was that other rifleman from down below? The one with a heavy-caliber Sharps from the sounds of it. Maybe a .50. Who did he know of that had one in this country?

That wolfer, Pike Moore, Hayes suddenly remembered. He sweated profusely. If it was Moore, then he could count Tucker out of this fight. And by now that mountain man might be working around and right above him!

Al Hayes knew a sudden wash of panic. He could not wait any longer. He uncoiled and suddenly burst from cover.

April's carbine lashed out. Dust jumped behind the low-hunched outlaw. He made two swift strides and a bullet kicked dirt at his heels.

This served to spur him to an even faster gait. Another bullet whipped past his nose, but he was almost across the opening.

Hayes suddenly knew he was going   to make it! His legs pumped harder.

Dan heard the sudden burst of firing from April's position. Now what did that mean? He edged forward.

April's rifle sounded again. Dan hazarded a look. His mouth flew open in astonishment. He fell back a half stride.

The little, evil-faced outlaw was almost upon him. A pistol, looming bigger than the man, protruded from his extended arm.

Dan Martin's teeth clicked together. A coolness that he did not realize he could command took hold of his brain. His own Colt swept up.

There was no time to think, nor to be frightened. His finger curled around the trigger. Dan fired once The outlaw stopped in midstride. His gun sagged and went off spewing dirt over his boots.

Baleful eyes glared at Dan. The little outlaw willed his gun arm to rise.

Dan fired again. The Colt bucked against his palm. A thin flame shot from the muzzle, followed by a drifting stream of blue-black powder smoke.

He could see dust jump from the rustler's shirt. The big .45 slug drove the man back and down. He slid to the trail below and lay curled on one side as if only asleep.

Chapter Seventeen

Dan Martin staggered back and sat down on a flat rock. A gut-wrenching sickness tore at his lean stomach. For one more time he knew the aftereffects of violence.

He mopped at his haggard countenance. His hat lay several feet away. But he hesitated to retrieve it, for he did not think his weak and trembling legs would support him just yet.

A hawk circled high overhead. Fleecy white clouds floated lazily above the graceful bird. The lowering sun cast a quaint beauty over the high-rising mountain peaks.

But Dan did not see any of this. Now he knew for a certainty. This business of being shot at and having to kill or be killed was not for him.

The first thing that he would do upon returning to Raton, Dan decided, as he fought down the constricting nausea in his throat, would be to wire Captain Franklin that this trouble was all settled. And his resignation would be included in the message.

Dan recognized his limitations. He had proved to himself that he was no coward. Just not that good with a six-gun, he thought sourly.

What if something like this happened again? Next time he might not be so lucky as to have along such a capable man as Pike Moore.

And he had better not forget April. For she had held up her end most admirably.

Dan vaguely realized that he still held the Colt in his hand. He eyed the lethal weapon for several moments. Finally, he stirred and shucked out the spent hulls.

The shiny brass cartridges lay at his feet. He thumbed in fresh rounds. Slowly it dawned upon him that he had shot the Colt dry.

A miss on that last go-around and he might be the one dead. A long shudder racked his frame.

Dan glanced up as a shadow fell over him. Not far away he could hear boots crunching on the gravel.

Pike Moore stood leaning on his long-barreled Sharps. "Easy, boy," he said. "This melee is just about wrapped up."

"I'm sure glad of that," Dan replied. He rose, finally trusting his wobbly legs to hold his weight.

April rounded the boulder. She looked questioningly at Dan and stooped to recover his hat. A fleeting smile touched the hard corners of her mouth.

"That was a pretty close call there, cowboy." April poked a finger through the bullet hole in Dan's hat before she handed it to him.

"Pike, how bad did the herd scatter?" she asked.

"Well, the shootin' boogered them some, but they're too tired to go far. Sounded like they ran out and quit when they hit that draw down there." He waved back along the trail.

"I heard three or four shots a short time back. Sounded like that rustler that got away run into somebody," Pike added. A thoughtful expression covered his homely face.

"Might be some of the Circle B outfit," April said. "I saw some of their stock in the herd."

"Uh-huh. It just could be," Pike agreed. "Well, anyway, it's too late in the day to try and round up them critters. I don't figure they'll go anywhere tonight."

"If anything, they'll just drift back towards their home range," April stated.

Pike nodded. "Dan, we got a disagreeable chore to do. Think you feel up to helpin' me bury these rustlers?"

Dan, although pale of face, had finally settled his jagged nerves. "Let's get it over with," he sighed.

Adam Brewer trailed the stolen stock with ease. He crossed a small meadow and found where several hundred head had been held for a short time. Adam studied this development and knew its implication.

This was now no small, isolated raid just on his range, but a full sweep of the Rafter W's north ranges as well.

The trail led out broad before him. Adam followed the combined herd for several miles.

Something kept bothering the big rancher. A set of fresh horse tracks overlay the trail of the cattle.

Just before full dark cast its cloak of gloom over the range, Adam neared a rough-mouthed canyon. The trail continued onward. Trampled-down brush widened the canyon's entrance.

He reined aside and found where the other

rider had also veered away from the canyon and dismounted. He gave the boot prints a cursory glance. Run-over heels, one sole cracked. From their size and shallow depth, they were made by an average-sized cowboy.

The stub of a burned-out cigarette was ground into one blurred print. Adam studied this, but could not supply a ready answer.

"He's trailing the herd, but he didn't stop for long," Adam muttered. "Wonder if he headed up that canyon? Be a dang fool stunt to rush in there now."

He ground hitched his mount and tracked the rider on foot, bent low to see in the dim light. Suddenly, the tracks cut off at a sharp angle.

"Huh?" Adam straightened to look off to the west. "Quit the trail and fogged it out of here in a hurry. Now I wonder where he is heading? There's nothing that way except a line shack. Nobody there either, according to May."

Adam slowly retraced his steps. He scooped up the reins in one huge fist.

"Come on, horse. We'll dry camp off the trail a ways. Take up the trail in the morning." He talked to himself as much as to his horse.

A cold biscuit and some jerky provided him with a frugal supper. He washed this down with a drink from his canteen. Moments later he lay wrapped in his blanket. His saddle made a pillow. Within minutes, a soft snore sounded from the lumpy bundle.

The waning moon cast a yellow light. Nearby, a cricket chirped. Adam rolled out of his blanket wondering what foreign sound had awakened him.

He swept up his rifle and padded quietly to where his horse was picketed.

The big Morgan steed's ears were pricked. He faced the trail. His nostrils flared.

"Ho, easy, boy," Adam soothed the beast. He clamped a big paw over the animal's quivering nose.

Dry brush crackled along the trail. Swift-thudding hoofbeats grew louder, drove past Brewer's position, then slowly faded in the distance.

"Heading for Raton, I bet," Adam murmured. "Must be one of the rustlers. Now I sure do wonder about this whole business." He patted the Morgan affectionately on the shoulder.

"Good thing I didn't ram on up that canyon. I'd have run smack-dab into him. And maybe the others also."

He leaned the rifle against his saddle and

rolled back up to sleep for a while longer.

The late morning found Adam Brewer high up in the canyon. He paused only briefly to study the outlaws' cold campfire.

This was a strange section of the range for him. Now he rode with extreme caution. The rifle rested across his saddle horn.

Several things still worried him, though. Who was the first rider and why had he suddenly turned west?

He puzzled over the second. Now why in the world would a rustler for some reason quit a drive and double back the same way that he had come? That did not make any sense.

He thought long on this and could not make heads or tails out of it. Finally, he gave up with a shrug and turned his full attention to the trail ahead.

A pass, he knew, cut through the mountains somewhere up ahead. But just how much farther to it, he didn't quite know.

Adam forged on deeper into the canyon. The Morgan took the rough going in stride.

Along about midafternoon the canyon suddenly peetered out. Its deceptive incline had gradually risen until Adam rode out onto a timber-studded mesa before realizing it.

The wide trail pointed straight ahead. Broken brush and small saplings, trampled by the herd, pointed due north like an accusing finger.

Even if sharp hooves had not left their trace in the grassy mesa, these scarring marks made for easy tracking.

The Morgan paced along easily. He soon crossed the small mesa. Horse and rider dipped down into a rugged but wide draw. The trail they followed continued up its gravel-strewn bottom.

Adam reined in and cast a speculative glance along the sides of this ragged arena. A thin stand of lodgepole pines grew on both banks. They spread up for several rods before the walls flattened into rock-studded buttresses.

Uncombed brush grew thick and rank along both banks. But it quickly thinned to allow easy riding up within the timbered area.

Adam chose not to ride openly up the draw. He reined aside and sent the Morgan up the left bank.

Soon they were weaving through the timber. The Morgan's hooves whispered over the matted needles.

Gunshots racketed some distance up the draw. The spiteful crack of a Winchester was almost lost in the loud popping of several heavy-caliber handguns. A large-bore rifle overrode even these.

The startled Morgan shied, almost unseating his rider. His head came up, ears forward and nostrils flaring.

Adam hauled up on the reins. He quieted the nervous beast and sat listening, trying to judge the gun battle.

The big rifle sounded once more, followed by the lone Winchester's thin report. An uneasy silence fell over the mountains.

Adam waited several minutes before he gigged the restive Morgan into motion. He rode slower, now paying closer attention to the trail ahead.

Bud Stone slashed his laboring mount viciously across the head. He drove long-shanked spurs into the mustang's laboring barrel, striving to gain more speed from the near-spent horse.

Horse and rider crashed through a tangle of brush and broke into a meager clearing. The mustang stumbled and went down hard, throwing his rider into the waist-high grass.

Stone landed and rolled catlike to his feet. He tried to jerk the heaving pony up, but could not.

Stone roundly cursed the worn-out mustang. He gave up his futile efforts and spun around to run for the covering timber.

The scared outlaw took one step and stopped stock-still in his tracks. His eyes bugged wide.

Adam Brewer sat high astride the Morgan. He loomed ominously over the panting rustler. The wicked muzzle of his Winchester centered on Stone's chest.

"Don't try it," Adam cautioned. He eased back the hammer.

But his warning did not stay Bud Stone's quivering hand. The outlaw gave way to complete panic at being captured.

A clawing hand fisted the black-butted Colt that rested along his leg. Bud could not think clearly in his frightened state.

Moisture drenched the rustler's pale face. His sweaty palm clenched around the Colt.

The weapon cleared leather and for a brief instant Stone knew a lifting excitement. He was gong to beat the man on the black! Outdraw his already-pointing rifle!

The Winchester spit flame. Smoke drifted upwards from the muzzle.

Stone felt a tearing pain rip apart his shoulder. The heavy impact jolted him back and down. The Colt flew spinning from his nerveless hand.

He was staring at the blood that flowed down his arm. A shocking realization tore at his mind. Captured!

Chapter Eighteen

The campfire burned low. Adam Brewer looked across the glowing embers to put a studied gaze on the haggard-faced outlaw.

Stone lay sleeping on a blanket. There was no need to tie him up.

"Pike, do you reckon he'll make it?" Adam asked.

"I think so," Moore answered. "He lost quite a bit of blood, but the bullet went through clean. He'll probably be crippled. Hard to say."

"That'll keep him from swinging a wide loop," April said, joining the conversation. "Anyway, he won't need two good arms where he's goin'."

"That was a mighty interesting story he told about Ross and Buck Shedd. Captain Franklin and the governor will sure be glad to hear it," Dan chipped in.

Pike grinned much like a hungry wolf. "Amazing how quick a man will spill his innards when he thinks he's the guest of honor at a necktie party."

"Would you have really strung him up if he hadn't talked?" April asked.

"Naw. But he sure did think so," Pike replied.

Adam Brewer's pensive stare shifted to April. "You know, Ross had a right smart idea about this timber. It will pay us to look into setting up a sawmill ourselves."

April agreed. "There's no real good market for beef anymore. Too many farmers and small outfits takin' over. What do you think, Pike?"

That worthy spat. "Why not?" he asked. "Sounds like just what this area needs. Well, it'll be a hard day tomorrow. I'm for turnin' in."

Dan agreed heartily with that suggestion. "It's been some day." He rolled up in his soogans and fell into a troubled slumber.

* * *

Jack Lester shoved a bawling jag of Herefords into the herd.

He quartered around the milling cattle to meet Adam Brewer.

Dan drifted out of the timber and cut towards the two riders. He felt better straddling one of the outlaw's cow ponies. "Pike and Jasper are coming in empty-handed also," he said. "It looks like we just about rounded up all the herd."

April hove into view trailed by two Rafter W cowhands. At Adam's wave, she joined the group.

"Doctor figures that the rustler can be moved without killing him," Adam said.

"Good," April said. "Let's head this bunch home."

"You bet, Miss April." Jack Lester started to wheel his mustang away. He jerked up on the reins at April's next words.

"You tall drink of water. I'll talk to you later." She frowned. But a glint of good humor sparked her eyes.

Lester thought, Oh, no, I'm in for it now. But a sudden smile broke across April's face. It drove away the studied frown. She looked quite human. Even nice.

A chuckle escaped Pike Moore's whiskery mouth. Mirth crinkled the corners of his eyes.

Understanding burst over Lester. He beamed and gigged his mount into action. April had been tamed!

A lone rider met the slow-moving herd just above Turkey Creek. He fell in beside Pike and April to ride a short distance with them.

After he eased back to flank the herd, April motioned for Brewer to join them.

"Raines had plenty of good news," she said. "Shedd tried to kidnap Summer and got ventilated for his trouble. Looks like that just leaves Ross to worry about now."

"That is some news," Adam said. "Did he happen to swing by my place?"

"Yes. May said to tell you that your rider is sitting up and is goin' to be just fine."

"Good. That sure relieves my mind on that score," Adam said.

Spring Winters paced the bunkhouse porch. "May, what is happening?" she asked. Her worried gaze spanned the sun-drenched Circle B ranch yard.

"Don't fret so, Spring," May tried to reassure her sister. "Chuck didn't find anything amiss at the ranch." She did not add that Dan Martin's bedroll and warbag were gone.

"I know, but he didn't find any sign of Dan, either. Do you think he went after the rustlers?"

"He might have, although I don't see how he could have known about them," May answered.

"Oh, he said that he was going to trail April and see how that turned out. I'm afraid he may have run into them somewhere on the range."

"Be patient," May advised. "I feel things will be just fine." She hid a deep-seated worry of her own.

Autumn emerged from the bunkhouse. A glad smile lighted her rather full lips. "Wes is sleeping easy now," she announced.

Her eyes drifted northward. "Riders coming. Looks like Adam in the lead."

May shaded her eyes against the sun. "Yes, it is." A relieved sigh was quickly chased by an even more welcoming happiness at seeing the big figure sitting solid atop the black Morgan. "I see April and Pike," she added.

Raines and Lester trailed the three riders into the yard. May waited, tense and quiet, until Adam swung down and embraced her.

A flush of pleasure reddened May's face. Her wide-eyed stare held upon April's huge grin.

Pike Moore swung down from the back of Carl Tucker's chestnut. He noted Spring leaning weakly against the bunkhouse wall.

Two long strides put him at the young woman's side. He placed a gentle hand on her shoulder.

"Brace up, Spring. Dan is with the herd. He came through without a scratch."

Spring felt faint so great was her relief. A tiny "oh" escaped her lips.

Adam spoke. "We'll hold the herd on Turkey Creek tonight and the boys can cull it later. Right now we need to head into Raton and take care of Mr. Stanley Ross."

May looked puzzled. "Ross is dead. Buck Shedd ran Hawkins out of the store late yesterday, and when he went back, he found Ross in the office, shot through the chest. Marshal McCoy figured that it had to have been Shedd."

Pike Moore cast a hard look at Brewer. "With that outlaw, Stone, spilled and Ross bein' dead, this deal is all wrapped up."

"Roped and hogtied in a neat package," Adam agreed.

* * *

April winked across the supper table at May. "Now that you and me are hitched, and June ran off with Jack, that leaves Spring next in line."

May kept a straight face. She followed April's lead. "Then Summer comes next. She told me there's no way that Chuck Raines is getting out of it, either. Especially after that shooting."

"Uh-huh." April seemed to consider. She cast a serious study over Spring's flushed features.

"But not that good-for-nothin' poor excuse for a cowboy, Dan Martin," April continued. "Reckon you and me will just have to pick out a good man for Spring."

"Yes. She does seem to have trouble picking one out," May joined the baiting.

Spring bounced out of her chair. "Not you too, May?" she cried. "I thought you were with me in this."

The blood drained from Spring's face. Her eyes snapped and sparkled in the lamplight as her anger rose. She spun and rushed out of the room.

April covered a snicker. May nearly fell out of her chair, laughing.

"Do you think we went too far?" May choked.

"Naw," April replied, still trying to suppress

her mirth. "They'll run off for sure now. And want to help them."

Dan eased around the dark rambling ranch house. He led two saddled and ready-to-travel horses.

Darn the luck, he thought. Just when he was beginning to think that April would accept him, things went sour.

A note from Spring was crumpled in his vest pocket. The hour was late.

If April didn't like it, too bad, he figured. Dan rapped softly on a window.

Suddenly, it was flung open and April stood framed in flaring lamplight. Spring, dressed to ride, leaned against May.

Spring's pale face held a bewildered expression. Dan gritted his teeth. This was just too much to endure.

But April Winters could stand the suspense no longer. The woebegone look on the cowboy's face triggered her laughter.

Tears of mirth rolled down April's cheeks. "Spring, I'll give you a cowboy," she roared.

May's tinkling laugh echoed in his ears. "Good luck, you two. April just had to give Dan one last rawhiding!"